BLINDSIDED

Visit us at www.boldstrokesbooks.com

By the Author

Harmony

Worth the Risk

Sea Glass Inn

Improvisation

Mounting Danger

Wingspan

Blindsided

BLINDSIDED

by
Karis Walsh

2014

BLINDSIDED
© 2014 By Karis Walsh. All Rights Reserved.

ISBN 13: 978-1-62639-078-2

This Trade Paperback Original Is Published By
Bold Strokes Books, Inc.
P.O. Box 249
Valley Falls, NY 12185

First Edition: August 2014

CREDITS
EDITOR: RUTH STERNGLANTZ
PRODUCTION DESIGN: SUSAN RAMUNDO
COVER DESIGN BY SHERI (GRAPHICARTIST2020@HOTMAIL.COM)

Acknowledgments

Blindsided was written while I was in transition from Washington to Texas, and I'd like to thank all the people who helped make the move and the writing easier for me.

Thank you to Mom and Dad for wandering around Evergreen's campus while I took notes for this book.

Thanks especially to Dad for driving cross-country with me through snow and hail and lightning, and to Susan for sharing the adventure of driving two thousand miles with two goats and a cargo van. I cherish the memory of both trips.

Thank you to my editor, Ruth Sternglantz, for her encouragement and understanding of my scattered obligations during this time. As always, thank you to Rad, Sheri, and the BSB staff for binding my words in such a beautiful book.

Most of all, thank you to Cindy for every minute of hard work she put into making a home for me and our furry kids here in Texas.

Dedication

To Cindy
For bringing me home.

CHAPTER ONE

Welcome to the Shelton home of Chuck and Linda Baer, a truly inspiring couple who have devoted their lives to an ever-growing family of adopted children." Cara Bradley paused for a moment while the camera panned to the right and focused on the rambling house behind her. She turned and followed the unblinking stare of the lens, smiling as half a dozen kids— including two on crutches—spilled out of the doorway, right on cue. Even though they had made the same entrance several times, they seemed unrehearsed and happy. Cara's smile of response came almost reflexively since she had been in front of a camera since birth, but she felt it stretch from a rehearsed expression to a wide grin as the kids came bounding toward her. She was so accustomed to the film-ready smile that she sometimes forgot it wasn't her real and spontaneous one until moments like these snuck up on her.

"Cut. Got it." George Zimmer made some adjustments to his camera while he spoke without looking at her. Cara was used to his single-minded focus while on location. He'd talk to her and her producer, Sheryl McCutcheon, but his whole world narrowed to the size of the small glass lens. He rarely seemed to see beyond it until they were back in the van. She had picked these two for her team because they were so dedicated to the work they did. "Let's get some more footage of you listening to the music."

"Okay," Cara said. She linked arms with the oldest Baer child, a sixteen-year-old girl named Alissa. She was blind in one eye and had been adopted from Mexico only a few years earlier. She seemed much older than her age, with a serious but quick mind. Cara walked toward the house with her, mentally reviewing the names and native countries of the other Baers. There were eleven in total, from Alissa down to baby Ang Li, and Cara didn't want to accidentally mix up names when she spoke to them.

"Do we need to play again?" Alissa asked. She and her two brothers had played some jazz pieces for Cara during her last visit, a little over a week ago. Cara had expected them to be good—after the glowing recommendation from their school music teacher that the kids be featured on Cara's show—but she had been unprepared for the level of talent she had witnessed. They had not only displayed proficiency, but musicality as well, playing formal compositions and improvising with equal ease.

"No," she said as they walked into the dim interior of the house. George and Sheryl pushed past her and started setting up lights in the faded living room. "Your performance was perfect the first time. Some of our film was damaged, so we just need to get some more shots of me, and George will edit them in later. I remember the music and can pretend I'm listening."

Maybe the trio's performance hadn't been perfect, but it had been moving and free of self-consciousness or worry over making mistakes. Cara would have enjoyed listening again, but having two different recordings would make editing more difficult. She stood next to a large curio cabinet filled with dusty plaques and trophies—the frozen players on top of each one attested to the variety of sports represented—and let Sheryl fuss with her hair and makeup. The Baer clan settled onto the mismatched green sofas and love seats as if they were about to watch a show. Cara winked at one of the smallest children, and the little boy grinned at her, revealing a gap where his baby teeth had been. Cara was used to the disproportionately long time of checking lighting and sound and her appearance before filming a few seconds of footage, but to the kids the elaborate preparation must have made the filming seem as exciting and involved as a major motion picture. She wanted to assure them that she didn't like all the prep work and attention paid to how she looked, that it was only a necessary evil as she worked to share stories of love and hope in and around Washington's Puget Sound region, with her show's small audience. But she kept quiet and let Sheryl and George buzz around her as if they were about to shoot an Oscar-worthy epic. Because she wasn't really the star of this show. Today, the Baer kids were, and Cara wasn't about to deflate the excitement they were obviously feeling as the film crew invaded their home. She'd let them enjoy the limelight without giving in to her personal desire to downplay the process.

"As soon as each new adopted child is settled into the family home, Chuck and Linda begin exposing them to a variety of activities. When interest and aptitude overlap, the child is encouraged to pursue their chosen sport or hobby with dedication and commitment." Cara paused and looked at the display case beside her. She picked up a trophy with a gilded soccer player on top, leaving a dust-free rectangle in its place, and pretended to read the engraving before she returned her focus to the camera. "From soccer to sewing, baseball to bass guitar, these activities often become the ticket for each child's future success. There are already six Baer kids in college on full-ride scholarships." She relaxed while George shifted focus from her to the mementos in the cabinet, emphasizing the diversity of the kids' achievements.

Cara saw Chuck reach over and wipe his thumb across Linda's cheekbone. Linda's eyes were red with tears, and both parents cast looks of such love and pride around the room full of children that Cara had to glance away. She felt the typical tightness in her chest she always experienced when shooting one of her more heartfelt segments. She returned the trophy to the case, carefully aligning it with the dusty edges of the rectangle. Even as she admired the Baers and their talented children, a small part of her mind recalled innumerable interviews in her own childhood home. Her media-loving family had been all smiles and tears, affectionate touches and intimate glances. The results were so authentic-looking that even young Cara had fallen for them the first few times. Until she realized how quickly the affection turned to distance once the cameras were gone. The pretense of family unity had been just another self-serving act. Put on for show, for publicity.

Back to the present. More lighting checks, more makeup smeared across her cheekbones. She had to remind herself that the people around her weren't her family. Chuck and Linda weren't trained actors seeking publicity. As far-fetched as the idea often felt to Cara, the Baers seemed to truly want to spread their love as widely as possible. Cara tried to keep that in mind as she sat on the green-and-gold plaid recliner where she'd been placed during the kids' original jazz session. She leaned on her left elbow and crossed her legs at the ankle, mirroring the position she'd been in a week earlier. No cynicism was allowed to show on her face. Once George began filming, Cara replayed the music in her mind, letting her expression shift along with the remembered dynamics. The room was quiet and no instruments were played, but she heard each note and reacted with an appreciative nod during the bass guitar solo by Trevor, a spontaneous-seeming clap when J.J. finished an intricate riff on his sax, a slight sway of her upper body when Alissa led a particularly melodious section on the piano.

Her performance was refined and nuanced. Was it better than her unrehearsed responses when she had actually been listening to the music, with no preparation? Cara wasn't sure. Even when she watched herself in uncut footage, she couldn't see much difference between the moments when she was being her natural self and when she switched to her on-air persona. She was a pretty face on the screen, nothing more.

When she came to the end of the silent playback, Cara grinned and clapped as if she had just experienced a beautifully sung aria at the Met. The entire Baer family applauded after she did.

"Amazing," Linda said. "You have an excellent memory."

"And a great sense of rhythm," Chuck added. "You were tapping your foot during what I remembered was the second movement when J.J. improvised around the melody, and you kept time beautifully. I could almost hear him playing while I was watching you pretend to listen."

"Um, thanks." Cara felt an unaccustomed heat in her face at the praise. She was no stranger to glowing comments about her looks or her acting ability, but Chuck's and Linda's comments reached deeper somehow. They saw skills, where other people often saw only a hereditary and surface quality in her. She fought against that shallow type of judgment, so why was she more comfortable hearing compliments about her Bradley-family looks than these words about her unique and personal abilities? Maybe because she had a hard time believing her skills were unique.

"Are you a musician, too?" Alissa asked, perching on the arm of Cara's chair while George and Sheryl began clearing the room of tripods and lights.

"Not like you." Cara nudged Alissa gently with her elbow. "But I do love to sing. In the car, in the shower. Loudly and off-key, but with joy."

The family laughed, and Cara took the opportunity to change the subject. She made sure she talked to each of the children—focusing on the ones who hadn't been featured in the segment for her show—and asked about their hobbies and pets and favorite subjects in school. George moved around in the background and captured some of the conversation on film. This was Cara's favorite part of the production. The people she interviewed for her public television series, *Around the Sound*, were often stiff and hesitant to talk when the microphones and lights were pointed in their direction. But after most of the equipment had been moved away, and Cara nudged them into conversations about their passions, they became different people. Open and relaxed. One moment trying to play a part in front of the camera, and the next simply being themselves. Cara loved the clarity of the shift from camera-shy to authentic. She had been raised among trained actors who could play on or off camera with equal ease, so she had never been certain which reactions were true. She wasn't always sure whether her own behavior was real, half the time. But when it came to people like the Baers, these unstudied moments were the ones that made her show come alive to viewers. They made each story, and each interviewee, come to life for her.

All too soon, Sheryl waved her hand at Cara and pointed at her watch in a not-so-subtle reminder that they had another segment to film today, in the nearby town of Olympia. Cara extricated herself from the group of children that had gathered around her chair. She left with promises to keep in touch and waved out the window until the van had pulled out of the driveway and onto the main road.

Once they were out of sight, Cara took a new outfit off a hanging rod and started to change out of the clothes she had worn during the filming of the jazz session last week and again today for the reshoot. She tugged a yellow polo shirt over her head and tossed it on the seat behind her.

"So, what's the *real* story behind the Baer family?" George asked from the driver's seat.

Cara slipped her arms into a pale blue shirt and buttoned it while she thought. "You know those stuffed monkeys with long arms and Velcro on their paws?" she asked. "The ones people hang on their rearview mirrors?"

George poked at a brown-and-white monkey hanging beside him, making it sway. "I think I've seen them around. Somewhere."

"They're made in a sweatshop in the Baer basement." Cara wriggled out of her khakis and replaced them with a pressed pair of deep blue denim jeans. "The children spend their nights slaving away with needles and thread and polyester fiberfill. I'm pretty sure I saw at least one kid with Band-Aids on his fingers from working them to the bone."

"Always the skeptic." Sheryl laughed. "I wonder what you'll come up with for our next interviewee, Lenae McIntyre, the guide-dog trainer."

Cara raised her hips off the seat and zipped the snug jeans. "I'm not sure yet, but I smell a government conspiracy of some sort. Or perhaps she's secretly training an army of robotic dogs so she can take over the world."

Cara took her hair out of the ponytail she had worn for the Baer story. She combed it and caught a few strands from either side, securing them with a gold barrette. Her jokes about the scandalous truths behind the stories she filmed—always ludicrous and obviously fiction—were standard fare for the van ride home. She had originally started the routine as a way to ease the confusing ache she felt as she drove away from these places where people were acting out kindness and self-sacrifice in their daily lives. She went through the same gamut of emotions every time she filmed a new segment for her show. She'd get excited during the research phase and feel the swell of warmth during the shooting. But after, in a way she couldn't explain, the foundation of her emotions would crumble. She'd wonder if she'd been duped, or had missed some clue about the reality of the situation. Because people couldn't really live this way—connecting with and touching others, working tirelessly to protect people or animals or the environment with little thought to their own needs. Despite all the evidence to the contrary, she couldn't entirely stamp out her thought that people like the Baers—so proudly supporting the kids they'd adopted as their own—could actually exist. Her pure response to the stories she told was tainted by the nagging thought that once the crew drove away, the phony façade was dropped and people reverted to a self-centered state. She never stayed around long after the cameras shut off, so she didn't have any real frame of reference except for the memory of her own family.

Cara looked through her notes while Sheryl used a battery-operated curling iron on her hair. Yes, she always experienced this letdown after filming, but she kept going because of the hope that eventually she'd believe the inspirational stories she saw with her own eyes and on the television screen when she watched her show.

One thing she knew for certain: most of the organizations and individuals featured on her program received a definite increase in donations and volunteers after their segments aired. She might not have a huge audience, but she did reach dedicated viewers who shared similar values and beliefs with the people she spotlighted. They proved it with their time and money. As cynical as Cara often felt, she couldn't deny the statistics. The McIntyre Center was new and small, but Cara had heard about it through one of her students at Evergreen State College. His cousin had received a guide dog trained by Lenae McIntyre, and her entire life had changed. Cara's student had raved about his cousin's newfound freedom, the way her world had suddenly expanded, and the close bond already forming between her and her dog.

Cara had known immediately the story would be perfect for her. Her audience would love the animal angle, and the new center would benefit from the exposure. Lenae apparently hadn't sounded as enthusiastic about the possibilities when Sheryl had contacted her, but she would soon be convinced otherwise. Cara scanned the information about the training center and about its visually impaired founder, and she wondered—as she always did before a new story—if Lenae McIntyre might be the one to finally make her believe in the fairy tale.

Chapter Two

"You're off duty for now, Baxter." Lenae rested one hand on the retriever's back as she unbuckled his harness with the other. She felt him sink from under her hand as he plopped onto his bed. She reached down and rubbed his head where it rested on his forepaws, laughing at his loud sigh. She had heard that mothers of newborns were supposed to sleep when their babies did, so they got some rest. Baxter seemed to have his own version of the advice. Whenever Lenae paused during her hectic days—whether Baxter was near his bed or not—he immediately settled in for a nap.

Lenae stood and walked from her office to the long row of outdoor kennels bordering the training facility. Even with her slow and careful stride, she nearly tripped when she stepped on the tines of a rake. It fell with a clatter on the cement walkway, and she picked it up and returned it to its proper place. She'd have to remind Sara, the high school student who worked weekends at the center, about the importance of replacing all items in the exact same spot every time she moved them. Lenae was accustomed to the bruised shins and stubbed toes she got regularly, but soon there'd be a group of students here to work with their guide dogs for the first time. They needed the comfort and reliability of a safe training area.

Until they began to connect with their animal guides, of course. Once they were familiar with their dogs, they'd be able to handle increasingly challenging environments. But at first they needed safety and predictability. And Lenae herself needed order and sameness here, where she'd not only be working but also spending most of her free time. Even when she wasn't actively training her dogs, she'd be here checking on them or playing with them, as she was today. She needed to be able to walk through the kennels without worry. Today, especially, she needed to be comforted by the physical aspects of her training center. The dogs, the order, the routine. She felt unmoored by the changes about to occur, precipitated by a need to increase the community's awareness of her new center, and she had come to the kennels to reorient herself. She had chosen the dogs, had designed the layout of the center, and had drafted a five-year plan for building it into a thriving program. If she had to let a television crew invade her privacy for one afternoon in her quest to make the center a success, then she'd do it. Reluctantly.

Lenae unlatched the door to the first run and stepped inside. She lowered her hand until it came in contact with a soft muzzle and the greeting swipe of a wet tongue. She kept contact with the dog while she shut the door again, listening for the click of a secure latch and feeling to make sure the lock was firmly bolted. Then, once she was convinced they were locked inside, she knelt next to the dog and rubbed his soft ears.

Lenae chatted with the young animal while she felt his legs and body, checking for any sign of injury or discomfort and enjoying the warmth of contact. Toby was one of her trained dogs, ready for his first experience with a new vision-impaired owner, and he exhibited all the signs she wanted to notice at his level. He sat quietly while she poked and prodded. He pressed close to her, as if seeking to be in her space and comfortable having her in his. The occasional lick of his tongue or rub of his head maintained a connection with her. He would soon transfer his loyalty to the one person who would be his constant companion, but Lenae enjoyed his affection for now, even as she imagined him lavishing it on his welcoming new owner.

After spending a few minutes with each of the three trained and ready dogs, Lenae moved to the runs holding the five dogs that had just arrived for training. These animals greeted her more boisterously, as active and energetic as teenagers, and she was even more cautious about checking the latch behind her each time. She made certain the dogs didn't jump on her or push too roughly, but otherwise she didn't attempt to curb their enthusiastic responses to her presence. She petted and played with them, wanting them to enjoy the company of a human. Once their training started, they'd be taught to control their more exuberant tendencies while still letting their personalities shine through. While they were in this less-trained state—obedient to basic commands, but not overdisciplined—Lenae was better able to determine their individual characters. She'd form opinions about the type of person most suited to each, and although she occasionally changed her assessment during the more rigorous evaluation to follow, most often her initial impressions held true.

Regular interaction and play with humans was a requirement for these future guide dogs, but Lenae often felt she was making these rounds as much for her own benefit as for the dogs'. Even now, with the television filming looming over her, she felt the muscles in her chest and shoulders loosening. There was nothing like petting and playing with dogs to get her to relax those tightly wound muscles. The upcoming need to look friendly and chat with people who saw her and her center only in terms of ratings and photo ops was wearing her down, but still she went toward the last occupied run with an anticipatory smile on her face.

All of her dogs were important to her because they meant the training center had a chance of being a success. She had trained individual service animals in the past—whenever her busy work schedule had allowed—but now she was planning to do the work full-time. More than the future of the center, though, was the realization that each of these dogs would mean a sense of freedom and companionship for someone trapped in a lonely and restricted world. She loved having the opportunity to give other sight-impaired people the same experience she'd had when she first got Baxter. Her world had grown, physically and emotionally, when she had been handed the training harness and had first knelt to fumble through fitting it to the patient dog. She had expected to find in him a helper, a guide to get her around more easily and swiftly, but she had found so much more—a relationship with more depth and trust than she had ever experienced, more so than she thought would be possible with other humans. Funny that she needed a television program—the ultimate in meaninglessness, in her opinion—to help promote her efforts to provide deep relationships between her dogs and the people with whom they'd bond.

Lenae edged her way into the last run, counting puppies with one hand while she groped for the latch with the other. There seemed to be more than three of them as they tumbled over each other in the attempt to get closer to her. She finally got the door securely fastened, made sure she had the requisite number of pups still inside the gate, and sat down on the springy grass. She laughed as she was assaulted by the furious licks and eager wet noses.

Lenae picked up her personal favorite of the bunch, a Lab named Pickwick, and cuddled him close. She burrowed her face in his fluffy baby fur and felt his whole body wriggle because he was wagging his tail so hard. She let the warmth and softness of all three pups ease the tension she had been carrying all day. All of her training animals mattered to her, but these three—as well as three others from another litter that were still with their mother—had special meaning. They'd be the first group of service dogs to be in her training program from the very start. The dogs waiting for their new humans and the ones waiting to begin their first days of training were animals she had purchased from other facilities. These puppies would be with her from day one, and she'd be able to control every detail of their training, from puppy walking until they were released to their new owners. They were the real future of the center, and the true test of her methods and talent as a trainer.

And they were a huge responsibility. She'd need to make sure they went to the right homes, and that they received care and nurturing according to her exacting standards. The weight of the burden was frightening, but she had to accept it if she wanted to make a go of her dream. She was confident in her ability to train a dog and owner, but this was different. Her best chance of success was to follow the same methods she had used in other jobs—and in her everyday life. To try to control every detail so nothing tripped her up.

Lenae gave each puppy a final pat before she got up and put her hand on the chain-link fence, following it to the door of the run. She had given each of her animals some hands-on time, vital for their development, but she had been given something more. In her exhausting and never-ending search for funding and publicity for the center she had reluctantly agreed to be spotlighted on public broadcast television, but it seemed so at odds with the serious work she was trying to do. Spending time with the dogs, seeing them in the various stages of training and development, had made her recommit to the work she was doing. She hated to admit it, but she needed help promoting the facility. She had researched the TV show, hosted by Cara Bradley, after receiving the offer of a segment, and even though it was low-budget and local, it had a good following and would hopefully reach some potential donors and puppy-walking volunteers.

Lenae had spent enough time behind the scenes of television shows—national news broadcasts and not local feel-good programs—to be aware of the shallowness too often present in front of the camera. Today she would put herself in the spotlight for a brief moment and likely feed the host's desire to promote herself in the industry by acting caring and philanthropic while the cameras were rolling. This time with the dogs, especially the pups, had grounded Lenae. Reminded her why she was going through this today.

She managed to get out of the run without letting the mass of puppies escape, and she walked back to the office to get Baxter.

She needed him beside her during the filming. She knelt next to him and he immediately got up and moved so his back was directly in line with her hands. He practically put himself in the harness whenever she brought it near him. She was about to snap the lead on his collar when she felt a tremor of excitement run through him.

"Morning, you gorgeous creature. Oh, and hi to you, too, Lenae."

"Morning, Des." Lenae kept the lead in her hand. "Go on, Baxter. It's okay."

Once he had her permission, Baxter left her side. She heard his nails click across the floor and felt the energy and heard the grunts and laughter of Baxter and Desmond's daily wrestling match. Lenae had interviewed several applicants for the job of assistant trainer, but Des had been given Baxter's immediate stamp of approval. She was so attuned to her dog that she could sense whether his ears were up or down, or where he was looking. She had felt Baxter's happiness when Des had knelt to pet him—the enthusiastic wag of his tail and the relaxed posture of a dog completely at ease with someone. She hadn't hesitated to hire the young grad student, and since then she hadn't once regretted trusting Baxter's instincts. She knew her own weren't good enough, but his were unerring.

"Will you make sure the yard is presentable for the film crew?" Lenae asked when Baxter returned to her. She heard the steady rhythm of his panting as she clipped on his lead. "Oh, and we need to talk to Sara again about leaving things out of place. I'd have felt like a fool if I had tripped over that rake while they were filming the show."

"I'll take care of it," Des said. "You just concentrate on smiling for the camera and getting through the day. Keep Baxter by your side and he'll win the hearts of anyone watching."

"I wish Baxter could do the whole interview." Lenae stood and slid her hand along his back until her hand connected with the harness. She gripped the padded handle and felt the accustomed sense of rightness she always felt when joined to Baxter.

Des gave her shoulder a quick pat as he walked past her to do his own tour of the runs. "I'll let you in on a little secret. Baxter might be the brains of your little operation, but you're the beauty. With the two of you and that swarming mass of puppies, the donations will be rolling in."

Lenae was still smiling at the compliment when she heard Des leave the office. He was clearly aware of her reluctance to be on TV, but he seemed to think she was just camera-shy and had probably meant his declaration of her beauty to be a confidence booster. She didn't try to set him straight because it was easier to listen to his encouragement and advice than to tell him the real reason she had tried to avoid doing the show. She didn't mind standing in front of a camera—and the audience it represented— but she *did* mind being used for someone else's self-advancement. Cara Bradley was most likely looking for attention, for a chance to break into a bigger market, pretending to be interested in the people and stories she spotlighted, but only after one goal. Self-promotion.

Lenae had been used once, giving her heart to a woman only to realize it wasn't her heart Traci was after—and she never wanted to let anyone use her again. She had left her job as a television newswriter because she hadn't been able to determine the true character of the people she worked with. Now Lenae was far away from the shallow world of television, safely installed at her training center where she was surrounded by creatures she could completely trust. Having to allow her old world into her new one—even for a few hours—was disturbing, but she would put up with it for one day, for only one reason. This time, she wasn't the only one being used. She needed the publicity from the show, so she'd use Cara Bradley as well.

CHAPTER THREE

Cara watched out the window of the van as they approached the McIntyre Training Center and then drove around it to get the lay of the land. The freshly painted navy-and-white sign seemed to be the only new item on the property. Large dog runs covered nearly every inch of the patchy and weed-filled lawn that surrounded a faded gray prefab house. A training ring filled with a variety of obstacles was enclosed by a broken-down fence with chipped white paint. The big piece of property held promise, but it would require hours of work and buckets of paint before it looked really presentable. Cara heard George muttering to himself as he drove, and she knew he was trying to figure out what camera angles to use to hide the worst of the disrepair.

Cara had been reading Lenae McIntyre's bio during the ride. Feature writer for the Nation's News Network turned philanthropist and dog trainer. The story had all the right angles for Cara's show. Lenae had left a fast-paced, high-paying, high-profile job with Three-N for this significantly less lucrative and low-key new job. Even as Cara planned what to say when she was on-air and highlighting the sacrifices Lenae was making to help unite visually impaired people with service animals, she was wondering what Lenae was really getting out of this lifestyle change. Newcomer Three-N had quickly risen to be the most-watched cable news network in the country, and—given the dates she had been employed with them—Lenae must have contributed to its success. So why would she leave such a high-flying job for this shabby and run-down dog park? For the sole purpose of helping others? Cara doubted it. Maybe Lenae had made a critical error in her writing, exposed the network to liability, and left in disgrace. Okay, unlikely, since her research hadn't turned up any scandal. But Cara mentally filed the idea away. She could use it later when George asked for her semi-joking, cynical take on the story.

Cara got out of the van and approached the front door of the house, with its yellow sign indicating it was the office. The siding and front porch looked even worse close-up than they did from a distance. Yes, Lenae must have had a serious reason for leaving Three-N to come here. Cara's parents would have loved to have her working there—as an on-air personality and not a behind-the-scenes writer, of course—and they'd have had her involuntarily committed if she had tried to quit. But, much to their dismay, Cara had never wanted to be so exposed. She had her "little show," as they called it, and she was happy with the work she did even if no one in her family thought it was worthy of pride.

Cara was wrapped in thoughts of her family, and she was startled back to the present when a woman with a large golden retriever by her side opened the door just as she was about to knock. Lenae McIntyre.

Cara lowered her hand. "Oh, hello. I was going to knock, but you answered." She cringed at her inane way of stating the obvious. She rarely was at a loss for words, having been raised to speak in public as soon as she had uttered her first syllables, but the woman in front of her made it difficult for Cara to breathe properly. She was no stranger to compliments about her own looks, and therefore she disregarded any such praise as meaningless and no real indicator of worth, but Lenae was so stunning that Cara wanted to thank her just for standing there.

"I'm Cara Bradley," she said, smoothing out her expression with the skills of much practice, even though she knew Lenae couldn't see the subtle changes. Cara had a feeling Lenae was adept at discerning nuances of tone, and Cara's calmer demeanor would lead to a more controlled voice. Relax the muscles along the side of the nose, expand through the temples. Cara, after spending hours listening to her parents' advice and studying herself in the mirror, had developed some effective little tricks for keeping her face calm even when turbulent emotions thrashed under her skin. And Lenae definitely was getting under her skin. She was tall and poised, as if she was completely in control of every muscle in her body. Cara's mom would have called her statuesque. Lenae would have been as at home in front of the camera as she must have been behind the scenes as a writer. Her appearance was stylish, in a simple, classic manner. Dark mahogany hair in a bob, cut slightly longer in the front. A royal-blue button-up Oxford shirt with dark khaki pants. Cara wasn't sure whether Lenae had chosen her look because it was simple or because it flattered her, but it managed to do both. Sharp cheekbones were emphasized by the hairstyle, and the shirt highlighted her elegant figure. The colors would look well on camera, and they even brought out the brassy tones in the retriever's coat.

"I'm Lenae McIntyre." Lenae held out her hand and felt strong, warm fingers take hold of her own. No hesitancy or fumbling for grip, as Lenae so often experienced when shaking hands with someone for the first time. Her hand found Cara's naturally.

"Nice to meet you, Lenae."

Lenae pulled her hand away more sharply than she intended. Cara's use of her name—spoken in that oozing-honey voice of hers—brought conflicting feelings to the surface. Attraction, yes. But more than that. From the feel of Cara's hand fitting so perfectly in hers to the voice that could convince a person of just about anything, Lenae felt physically aroused even as she heard warning Klaxons in her mind. If Cara's looks were any match to her voice, she'd be a knockout. Definitely on the track to bigger and better media jobs. Lenae had been fooled by soft voices and the smoky sound of her own name spoken in ways she thought had been meaningful, only to find they had merely been self-serving. She didn't trust herself to judge by sound alone how much of Cara was practiced media personality and how much was the real person.

While Cara introduced her producer and cameraman, Baxter moved from Lenae's side until he was standing protectively in front of her legs. He was relaxed, but slightly on the defensive. Lenae put her trust in his instincts yet again. He seemed to think she needed protection, so she would close her ears to the sweet and sultry sound of Cara.

"Why don't you give us a tour of your center while we talk," Cara said. "Once George has seen his options, we'll return to a few of the places and fill in some of the gaps in the interview. Can you start by introducing me to this handsome fellow?"

Lenae relaxed fractionally when the attention turned off her and onto her dog. She could hear the sounds as George adjusted the camera, and she felt the presence of the boom above her head. Filming had already begun. "This is Baxter," she said, reminding herself why she was doing this interview. For the center. For all the people and dogs that would come through her doors and be forever changed by their new partnerships. "He's a five-year-old golden retriever, and we've been together for three years."

"It's customary to ask permission from the handler before approaching and petting a service animal," Cara said, her voice becoming a touch more distant as she addressed her remark to the camera. Lenae felt an odd sense of loneliness until she felt the whisper of Cara's breath and the focused sound of her voice when she faced Lenae again. "Is it all right if I pet him?"

"Yes, of course." Lenae dropped Baxter's harness so he knew he was free to visit. She wasn't sure how he'd respond to Cara since he had been initially protective of her, but she had complete faith in his polite manner. Even if he didn't like Cara, he wouldn't snap or be anything but gentle. To her surprise, though, the moment he was released and Cara knelt next to him, Lenae felt a quiver of excitement run through his body—even more pronounced than it had been when he met Des. She had been expecting him to be standoffish, but she felt him squirm like a puppy under Cara's attentions. Maybe he had only been reacting to Lenae's emotions, not responding to Cara's character as Lenae had originally thought.

More distracting yet was the sound of Cara's laughter, as seductive and sweet as her voice had been. She spoke to her television audience while she played with Baxter and got what sounded like a thorough licking. The laughter *sounded* genuine, but Lenae wasn't sure whether it really was.

Finally Cara stood up again. "Let's get a mic on you for the rest of the tour."

Lenae was accustomed to being touched by well-meaning but intrusive people who wanted to help her. She usually avoided any contact that made her feel weak or helpless—and that was most of the contact she faced on a daily basis. Department store clerks who wanted to assist her and often were too intimate with their touch. Other grocery shoppers who saw her feeling for items and stepped in before she had a chance to take care of herself.

Cara's touch was different. Respectful and minimal, although it generated a sensation of heat along Lenae's collarbone and against her belly when Cara clipped the equipment in place. Cara was dangerous. She seemed to know how to use her voice to seduce and charm. She left a trail of electricity everywhere her skimming fingers touched. She even had Baxter enamored of her. But she was still dangerous. She could lead Lenae to believe everything she said. She had already stirred up Lenae's arousal until she compliantly let Cara take charge of the mic even though Lenae had used one before and could have wired herself up in less time. Every place where Lenae had the potential to be weak, Cara was strong.

❖

Cara finished clipping the mic to Lenae's shirt and then she stepped away. Usually Sheryl took care of this small chore, but Cara had stepped in and done the job herself because she had been the one talking—the familiar one—to Lenae, and she thought the requisite touching might be less disturbing from her. But the second her fingers brushed the smooth, pale skin just above the waistband of Lenae's khakis, she had to admit that she had wanted to find out if Lenae's body lived up to its promise.

It did. Cara finished the job as quickly as possible, while still being sure to ask Lenae's permission each time before she touched her. She stayed silent on the short walk to the dog kennels behind the office even though she knew she should be chatting with Lenae to get some possible filler for the segment. Instead she gave herself a short break while she brought her focus off the three-dimensional world that included the feel of Lenae's skin and back to the two-dimensional world of appearances and videotape.

"I thought we'd start with the puppies," Lenae said when they reached one of the dog runs. Cara forgot her discomfort with Lenae's closeness once she saw the writhing mass of fur and fluff through the chain-link fence.

"Do you mind taking care of the gate, Cara? Be sure it closes behind us so no one gets out." Lenae told Baxter to stay before moving her hand along the fence until she reached the latch. She opened the door and slid through the narrow space and into the run.

"Of course. George can film through the chain link." Cara thought Lenae's words had sounded less like a request for help and more like a warning not to be stupid and leave the gate open. She sidled through the door, latched it securely, and immediately dropped to her knees next to Lenae. She had loved meeting Baxter, but the pups were something else. She ignored the rolling film and the script for her show for a few moments while she burrowed into the pile of puppies and tried to pet them while they licked and jumped all over her. She'd always loved animals but had never been allowed to have a pet while growing up. Animals were unpredictable and messy, not suitable at all for a family focused on appearances and putting on a show. Cara picked up a small chocolate Lab, clearly the runt of the litter, and snuggled him while he chewed on her carefully curled hair. There was no question of these animals being genuine and without artifice. Even Cara couldn't think a cynical thought when the pup looked at her with a clump of her hair sticking out of his mouth like a blond mustache.

Cara pulled her damp hair out of the puppy's mouth and fought to get her mind back on business and off play. "I'm holding a brown dog, the smallest one here," she said to Lenae. "What's his name?"

"That's Pickwick. He and his two siblings, along with another litter of three pups, will be the first to go through my training program from the puppy-walking stage to being matched with a visually impaired owner. It takes up to four months to train a dog and usually another month to get the partnership of dog and owner working smoothly, but the puppy-walking process takes a year or more before the dogs are ready for training. So it's vital that we have new crops of puppies entering our program on a regular basis."

Cara swallowed a sigh. Lenae spoke like someone who had written the right words to say, but who wasn't prepared to deliver those words with the persuasive entreaty needed to make people want to volunteer. "Who are these puppy walkers? Does the job require some special skills?"

"No. The main requirements are a safe place to raise the puppy and a dedication to exposing them to a variety of experiences." Lenae settled on the ground and lifted the other two puppies onto her lap. They seemed to have tired after their initial excitement, and they settled next to each other and wrestled halfheartedly. Cara watched Lenae's smile relax and deepen as she stroked the puppies. Despite her formal delivery, these dogs and the program obviously meant a great deal to her. Cara needed to do her best to bring some warmth to the story, and she summoned all her acting skills to do so.

"And what happens at the end of the puppy-walking stage?" Cara gave a sad frown to the camera, as if she knew the answer that was coming and found it difficult to face. She nuzzled Pickwick and he tried to bite her nose.

"Then the young dogs are brought into training." Lenae's voice seemed to grow colder as Cara increased the emotional response in her own. The opposite effect to what she had been trying to achieve, but Cara couldn't stop her own reaction at the idea of spending a year raising a puppy as if it were her own only to give it up without a second thought.

"Most people who have pets feel like they're part of the family. I guess it takes a certain kind of person to be able to just let them go without…being too sad about it."

Cara had been about to say *without caring* but stopped herself in time. She wasn't sure why the thought of someone so easily shuffling a puppy to a new owner made her gut clench. Maybe because she had often wondered—half in jest, even as a child—if her own parents would have hired a replacement to play their daughter if she herself hadn't been Bradley-pretty enough to look good in photographs. She and her brother Richard had laughed while spinning stories of being locked in the basement during their teenaged years while a more beautiful and less-acned duo acted in their place. But her parents hadn't been heartless enough to disown her even in her awkward stages. What kind of person would so casually dismiss a puppy?

"Yes, it does take a certain kind of person to be a puppy walker." Lenae answered Cara's spoken statement. She gently set her two pups on the grass and stood up. Baxter, as if sensing agitation in his person, came over to the door of the run and whined softly. "It takes someone with a lot of love and time to offer. It takes someone who understands the true meaning of the gift they're giving a visually impaired person. These individuals and families raise the dogs in a loving home environment, taking them to work and on errands, spending almost every hour of every day with them. They don't give them up after a year, but they give the dogs and their new owners a chance to have something special and wonderful together."

Lenae put her hand out and felt for the wall of the run, following it until she reached the door. She fumbled for the latch—obviously upset and shaken—before letting herself out and kneeling next to Baxter. She reached for him, and Cara saw the dog move until his head was under Lenae's seeking hands. Lenae stroked Baxter's face, and then she clipped on his lead and picked up the handle of his harness. She stood and faced in Cara's direction.

"If Lynn hadn't been willing to puppy walk Baxter, if she hadn't raised him in a place of love and human interaction, I'd never have the freedom I have now. I can go more places more easily, more independently, than I ever could before. But it's more than that. We're best friends and we watch out for each other. The trust between us is complete and unquestionable. Have you ever felt that kind of bond with any other being?"

Cara gave Pickwick a hug and set him next to his siblings. She stood and looked at the three people standing outside the run. Lenae looked defiant and angry, but her hand was trembling where it rested softly on Baxter's neck. Sheryl was looking between Cara and Lenae as if she wasn't sure whether or not to step in and stop them from bickering. George had lowered his camera, no longer filming since the discussion was obviously one they wouldn't use on the show.

"No," Cara answered softly. "I haven't."

She let herself out the door, careful to keep the puppies from following her.

"We'll have to reshoot the dialogue portion, but I got some good footage of the puppies," George said, as unconcerned about anything but the filming, as always.

Lenae turned her head in his direction, and Cara thought she saw a smile forming on her serious face, but it disappeared as quickly as it had come.

"What next?" Sheryl asked Lenae in a falsely perky voice. Cara had planned for them to simply move from kennel to kennel during the shooting, meeting each dog and discussing its level of training, but Lenae's next words caught her by surprise. She didn't like surprises on filming day.

"Before our fully trained dogs are matched with new owners, they go through a final test of guiding a blindfolded volunteer. We want to find out how they adjust to a different voice issuing commands. I thought we could blindfold Cara and have Toby guide her around a little."

CHAPTER FOUR

Lenae was relieved to hear Des approaching once they had left the puppy enclosure. She was used to hearing the occasional person voice their disapproval of guide dogs, and she wasn't certain why Cara's implied criticism of puppy walkers had hurt so badly. She tried to tell herself it was because she had hoped this television segment would bring more of the needed volunteers to the program, not alienate or discourage them from helping. She shouldn't be surprised that someone like Cara—accustomed to the media world—would only see the black-and-white version of the story instead of the complex emotional commitment of the people who devoted months to the puppies temporarily in their care.

"This is Desmond Carter, my assistant trainer," Lenae said as soon as she felt him stop by her side. "He'll help us get Toby and Cara ready for the demonstration."

Lenae stepped back while the television crew introduced themselves to Des and discussed the best strategy for filming the demo. She had been planning to take a more active role during the entire afternoon of filming, but she was relieved to be given a small break to get herself together. Baxter hugged her side while Des described the route Toby and Cara would take along the quiet streets around the center.

A light whiff of oranges and vanilla signaled Cara's approach. The scent reminded Lenae of the ice cream bars she used to enjoy as a child, when the summertime sound of the ice cream truck brought her running to the curb along with the other neighborhood children. Flavors as soft and sweet as Cara's voice. Too bad her words hadn't had the same qualities as the tone in which they were delivered.

"I'm sorry," Cara said. "I didn't mean to insult you or the people who volunteer with your program."

Lenae noticed that Cara hadn't said she was wrong about her assessment, just that she shouldn't have spoken her criticisms out loud. "We can't survive as a training center without puppy walkers. One reason I agreed to do this show was because I wanted to reach more potential volunteers, not drive them away."

"I know. And when we rerecord the two of us talking about puppy walkers, I'll keep my opinions to myself and let you steer the conversation. Okay?"

"Sure." Lenae knew she should be satisfied because she would get what she needed—positive exposure for her center. Why did she care whether Cara approved of the process or not? "Baxter, find Toby."

Cara watched as the retriever set off down the aisle in front of the runs. She followed along more slowly, trying to regain the detached composure she usually felt during filming. Even when she was moved or touched by one of her segments, she always felt the hint of her forthcoming drop in energy and hope. They rarely shot more than one segment of the program at a time, only doing two today because they had needed to reshoot at the Baer house, and she had let the return of cynicism that she always felt after filming color her response to Lenae and the center. That must be the reason why she had challenged Lenae about the puppy walkers instead of simply acting like an uninvolved reporter.

Another retriever, shorter and stockier than Baxter, was waiting at the gate of his enclosure, pressing his nose against the door and wagging his entire hind end. Cara couldn't help but smile at his enthusiasm.

Desmond grinned at her for the first time, perhaps noticing her response to the dog's greeting. He was tall and lanky, with hipster glasses and long hair. She'd seen him watching Lenae with a concerned expression since he had arrived on the scene, but Toby's energy seemed to be lightening his mood—hell, everyone's mood. Baxter's ears were perked and his tail waved gently, and even Lenae was smiling as she held her palm up to the chain link for Toby to lick.

"As you can see, our dogs are very excited about the work they do." Des spoke with the overly loud voice of someone unaccustomed to wearing a mic, as if he were trying to project his voice to a large and invisible audience. He had a harness and lead in his hand, and when he held them up, Toby spun in delighted circles. "If any of our animals in training don't seem to love the work, we'll find new homes for them."

"So you believe the dogs truly enjoy the work they do? They're not just trained to perform a certain way?"

Cara thought she heard a snort of derision from Lenae, but when she turned toward her, Lenae's face showed no emotion. Des cleared his throat.

"Without a doubt. If you study animal psychology, you'll discover that we're meeting important needs for animals like dogs that live in packs. They're given companionship and a family unit. Unlike most pet dogs, they'll be with their pack, their handler, nearly twenty-four hours a day. They have work to do that is challenging but well-suited to their temperaments. It'd be a fulfilling life for any creature, I believe. A close bond with another living being and a satisfying job. Love and a sense of pride and accomplishment."

Cara could understand the career part of Desmond's argument. She found the same sense of pride in her work, even though her family—and people familiar with her heritage— didn't seem to believe her show and teaching were as worthwhile as she did. As far as the bond with another creature? Cara didn't know if it was possible for her to ever trust and love someone else so unconditionally. Maybe she could with an animal, since their motives and affections were much more innocent and clear than any human's.

"What qualities make a good guide dog?" Cara changed the subject from the realm of anthropomorphism to more practical matters. She found it easier to switch back to her usual on-camera persona with Des than with Lenae. Why was that?

"They need to be friendly and bond easily with people, but the work they do also requires independent thinking because they can't obey commands that will put their handler in danger. Still, the dogs we train have varied personalities, just like people. A skilled trainer, like Lenae, is able to match dogs and people so they form true partnerships."

Des paused and looked at Lenae with an expression of admiration. Everyone, even Baxter and the other dogs, seemed to adore her, but Lenae seemed to be unaware of their regard. Cara didn't see the appeal, aside from Lenae's obvious physical beauty. She was clearly intelligent and passionate about the work she did—qualities Cara usually found appealing—but she had an air of aloofness Cara couldn't read. But Cara was a professional. She didn't need to understand Lenae as a person, or care that Lenae seemed to have the same disapproving air Cara's parents had. She just needed to share Lenae's story and do her part to help the center.

"Lenae, what characteristics do you use to match each pair?"

"We start with physical traits, like height and stride length." Lenae turned away from Toby's run and faced in Cara's direction. "I can determine some of this by walking with the people and dogs, but Des is a great help in this area. He can see peculiar tendencies in gait that I might not notice. More important, though, are the unique emotional needs of each personality. Energy levels, daily schedules, lifestyle." She paused and moved her right hand toward Baxter. Cara watched the dog move his head until the two connected.

"In some ways, I want the pair to be similar, and in others I want them to complement each other," Lenae said as she stroked Baxter's head. "I don't have a set formula, but after I've examined all the variables I…I guess I go with my gut feeling."

Lenae frowned, as if uncomfortable with the admission, and Cara wondered how difficult it was for Lenae to give up control and let her instincts take over. The sensitivity needed to match dogs and owners was something Cara hadn't expected.

"Do you think Toby and I will be a good match for the day?" Cara asked with a smile and a wink for the camera. She was curious about Lenae's analysis of her, although she doubted Lenae could know her beyond the careful performance she gave on film. Even Cara wasn't sure what else was there.

Lenae considered the question. Based on the sound of Cara's voice, she gauged her at a couple of inches shorter than her own five eight height. Cara's natural pace seemed a bit slower than her own. Toby would be a fine choice physically. But emotionally? Mentally? Lenae didn't have a clue. Was Cara as empty and self-serving as others Lenae had experienced in the media world? She had been abrasive during the talk about puppy walkers, but Baxter had taken to her quickly. Lenae couldn't figure out who Cara was inside, where the lens of the camera couldn't reach, nor did she know why she was devoting so much thought to the question. The only important things were the exposure for the center and the opportunity for Toby to have a new learning experience.

"You'll do fine for the day as long as you're able to trust your dog. That's the key element in any partnership."

Lenae knelt and put her arm around Baxter while she listened to Des give Cara a crash course in handling a guide dog. Cara's laughter sounded real as she practiced using the harness and following Des around the lawn, and Lenae had to fight her surprising urge to smile in response. Cara still didn't seem to be taking the experience seriously—and Lenae wondered if she took anything seriously—but Lenae had experienced this part of the process many times before, first with Baxter and later as she'd trained other pairs of dogs and owners. Laughter and a pretense of indifference were often used to mask fear, anxiety, or excitement. Once the harness was attached to a live animal, and the two were on their way without guidance for the first time, the seriousness of the situation finally sank in.

Lenae scratched Baxter under his chin and felt his rough tongue on her wrist. She had been apprehensive about getting a guide dog at first. Such a physical and glaring proof of her difference—anyone who saw her walking down the street with him would know she was visually impaired and judge her as helpless. Giving up control as they sped along the sidewalk. Trusting him without reservation. She had spent her first days of training being told repeatedly to stop trying to guide *him*. To stop fighting for control and to let him take her places. And once she listened to the advice and gave up her need to be independent, she had discovered that relying on Baxter didn't make her weak or helpless at all.

Lenae stood when she heard the short training session drawing to a close. Cara, unlike the future owners Lenae trained, wouldn't experience the same depth of partnership Lenae had found with Baxter. The demonstration walk would be too short, and Cara might not be able to—or need to—deal with the struggle to let go. But maybe she would be able to understand a little of what Lenae experienced every day. The limitations, the freedoms provided by a guide dog, the indescribable bond between two beings. And then, maybe she would be able to convey the experience to her viewers.

"Find Cara," she said to Baxter, and he led her a few yards forward and stopped. She put out her hand and brushed the sleeve of Cara's shirt before she felt Cara's hand close over hers. The same sense of connection Lenae had felt before. Instead of touch being a necessary—and unwanted—experience for her, the feeling of anchoring herself to Cara was similar to what Lenae felt when she petted Baxter. A physical attraction, especially to someone she was unable to read and with whom she had little in common, was at best a distraction from her goals and at worst a sure way to get hurt. She let go of Cara's hand.

"Once you have Toby in the harness, you'll ask him to find the Starbucks. Then say *forward* and he'll take you there."

"Wow, it's as if you trained him specifically for me. I was running late and missed my morning caffeine fix today." Cara laughed again, and this time Lenae let herself smile in response.

"It does seem to be one of the most popular destinations here in the Northwest. We train all our dogs to detect the scent of roasting coffee beans."

"Hey, you told a joke," Cara said in a quiet voice. "I wasn't sure you were capable."

The intimate feel of Cara's lowered voice was discomfiting. Lenae felt a small thrill when Cara spoke just to her, not for the whole audience to hear, and she didn't like her own response. "I can be hilarious when I'm talking to someone who isn't challenging my career and methods."

"Ouch. Point taken, but I was only asking questions my audience will want answered." Cara, still blindfolded, jumped when a wet nose pressed against her hand. She had still been feeling the tingle from Lenae's grip, and the new contact seemed to come out of nowhere. She groped around and found Toby by her side. He was twisting around her legs and the movement was disorienting.

"Try tuning in to your other senses," Des said. He gently took her hand and slid it over Toby's back until she felt the handle of the harness. "Toby startled you when he came close because you were concentrating on what you couldn't see, not what you could hear or smell or feel."

"You can get a lot of information through the harness," Lenae said. "What direction your dog is looking, whether he is on alert or relaxed."

Cara nodded and smiled since she knew the camera was trained on her, whether she saw it or not, but she didn't feel any of the things Des and Lenae wanted her to sense. She knew

Toby was next to her, and she felt him shifting in the harness, unlike the steady pressure she had felt when Des had been playing the dog and showing her what to do. She wasn't sure this was a good idea anymore, but she had no real reason to stop the filming.

"I'll walk alongside you while we're on the property," Des said. "Once we go outside the gate, I'll drop back and let Toby take over. And remember, he'll stop at each curb, both up and down."

"Um, okay." Cara stood quietly, feeling the soft brush of Toby's wagging tail against her hand where it rested on the harness.

"You need to give him some direction," Lenae said. "He'll stay there all day if he thinks that's what you want."

"Oh, right. Toby, find Starbucks." Cara's voice sounded uncertain even to her own ears. Would Toby bother to follow her commands? She cleared her throat and injected more enthusiasm into her tone. "Forward."

Apparently Toby didn't mind whether or not she gave her commands in a confident manner. Before she got the syllable *ward* out, he was walking briskly and pulling her along. She struggled to lengthen her stride and keep up even though every instinct in her was demanding she walk slowly and cautiously through the unfamiliar darkness from the blindfold.

"I'm right here," Des touched her right shoulder. "Relax your left arm and let him take up the slack in the harness. He's supposed to pull against you slightly."

Cara tried to loosen the taut muscles in the hand holding the harness, but she didn't want Toby to pull her anywhere. She wanted to pull him to a stop and catch her breath, take off the blindfold, go home. Great. She was having a meltdown.

"Relax, Cara. He won't let you get hurt."

Cara wanted to scream at Des that simply repeating the suggestion to relax wasn't doing her any good. She had lost all sense of judgment about speed and direction. She wasn't sure if she and Toby were race walking or going at what would have been her normal pace. Were they moving in circles or in a straight line? Cara's disorientation grew with each step until Lenae's calm voice broke through her increasing panic.

"Tell him to stop, Cara."

"Toby, stop." She winced at the desperate note in her voice and almost fell over when Toby came to an abrupt halt.

She felt Lenae's hand softly touch her forearm, sliding down until her fingers covered Cara's on the harness.

"Let go for a moment," Lenae said.

Cara opened her stiff fingers and felt Lenae's touch on the palm of her hand, where Cara was sure she had indentations from her nails. Lenae kneaded her hand for a moment, and then replaced it on the harness. Even in her distracted condition, Cara couldn't help her sharp inhale at the feel of Lenae's hand, at once soothing and electrifying.

"For now, hold the harness in an underhand grip. It'll keep you from hanging on so tightly. We need our dogs to pull out, but we don't pull back against them. Think of what you'd do if a little child grabbed your hand and wanted to take you somewhere. You'd hold her hand, but not pull."

Cara dropped the harness again. "I really shouldn't do this. I'm messing up all your training and—"

"Toby's new owner will be just as scared the first time they're together. Uncertain, unable to give control over to the dog. This is part of his training, and we often use blindfolded, sighted volunteers for this. You won't ruin him."

Cara wanted to protest and claim she wasn't afraid of this simple walk with a dog, but she couldn't lie. She wasn't afraid of getting hurt or looking foolish, but there was some unnamed anxiety associated with the feeling of flying through the world without any idea of what was beyond the wood-and-leather harness in her hand. She couldn't feel their presence, but she knew Sheryl and George were watching and waiting for her to perform for the camera. Toby gave a small whine as if he didn't know why they were just standing there and not romping through the streets of Olympia.

If Cara knew anything for certain, it was how to put on the right face for the occasion. "All right, let's try this again," she said with a grin. She had to assume George would adapt to her blindfolded state and move the camera so she was facing it. "It's an interesting, and admittedly scary, feeling to be guided without having any sense of where I am or what's around me. I'll put my trust in this dog that Lenae and Des have trained so well and work on expanding my awareness beyond what I can't see."

"That's how a true partnership develops," Lenae said. "Baxter doesn't just pull me around like a completely passive passenger. I'm doing my part by remaining aware of my environment with my other senses. We work together."

"I hadn't realized how much I relied on my sight until I didn't have it. Now I know what to expect." Cara took a deep breath. The break had given her time to catch her breath, but the only thing her senses were aware of was Lenae's closeness. The scent of Chanel, the throaty timbre of her voice. Sophisticated smells and sounds, but the softness of Lenae's touch was something grounded and down-to-earth.

"Toby, find Starbucks. Forward."

Cara did her best to focus on the parts of the world around her that she still could access. The moment when her shoes hit pavement instead of grass—making her thankful she hadn't worn heels for this frantic stroll—and the uncomfortably loud sounds of cars rushing by. Logically, she knew they weren't going fast on these suburban streets, but without her eyes to pull everything together into a cohesive whole, her surroundings seemed a chaotic mix of half-heard, half-understood noises and sensations.

"You're coming to a curb," Des said from somewhere behind her right shoulder. Cara prepared herself for a step down, exaggerating every footfall, before she remembered Toby would halt at curbs. Actually, she didn't remember until he stopped and she stumbled over the cement and into the street.

She was attempting to straighten up with some shred of dignity intact when she felt Toby move in front of her and push against her legs. She obeyed his subtle nudge, stepping back onto the sidewalk, when she felt the slight breeze and heard the vibration of a car passing in front of her.

"Ask him to go forward again, but wait for him to move," Des said, his voice sounding unaffected by what Toby had just done.

Cara asked Toby to move again. Every muscle in her body had felt tight with the need to have some control, some preparation for disaster, but the realization that the dog had stepped in and moved her out of danger distracted her enough so she was able to follow his lead more easily. They came to the next curb, and he paused again before stepping up. Cara followed numbly.

She had looked longingly at the neighborhood Starbucks when the van had driven past it earlier, but she still had no sense of where she was. She and Toby seemed to be taking the most circuitous route to get to the café, but all of a sudden he halted again.

"Forward, Toby," she said. When he didn't move, she felt with her toe for a curb or obstacle blocking her path.

"May I help you?"

Cara reached out and her hand bumped into a hard surface. Slowly, the noises and smells around her separated from the jumbled mass of sensations. The background buzz of conversations, the smell of brewing coffee and scalding milk. Toby had gotten her to Starbucks. She had been so closed to everything outside her own small and sightless world that she had failed to notice they had entered a building. Someone must have held the door for them, or she'd have probably smacked right into it.

"Grande pumpkin spice latte." Cara startled again when George spoke his order from right behind her. She had forgotten the small entourage traveling with her and Toby. "That was great footage, Cara. Can't wait for you to see it."

"Toby was looking out for you the whole time, even when you tried to get him to go forward into a garbage can," Sheryl added. "The audience will be able to see how he was thinking and making decisions for you."

The demonstration seemed over, so Cara pulled off her blindfold and looked around for Lenae. She was standing off to one side and talking to Des, with Baxter by her side. Cara let Toby's harness drop—remembering Des had said it was his signal that he was off duty—and she walked over to them.

"Thank you for the chance to film one of your dogs at work," she said, her voice sounding formal and detached even though her feelings were anything but. She couldn't voice what she wanted to say. That she now understood a tiny fraction of what Lenae experienced every day. Even though she was grateful to Toby and amazed at what he had done, at the same time she disliked the way George and Sheryl had made her sound like less of a person when they praised Toby for leading her so successfully. By taking her sight away temporarily, Lenae had given her a glimpse into a new world.

"You did a great job," Des said. He took Toby's lead from her. "It was a very successful trial for Toby."

"He's going to make a wonderful partner for someone." Cara rubbed Toby's head. "He stopped me before I fell into traffic at the first street we crossed."

Lenae laughed for the first time since Cara had met her. "Baxter had to rescue me several times during our first weeks together. I wanted to go my own way and had a hard time following his lead. At least you didn't fall down. I ended up on my ass in a mud puddle the first time he stopped at a curb and I didn't. My trainer, Angie, told me he just sat there and stared at me reproachfully until I untangled myself from the harness and got up."

Cara laughed as well at the imagined scene. "Baxter seems to be a very dignified fellow. I'm sure he was embarrassed by your somersault off the curb."

"And then he had to be seen with me in muddy jeans. We were both humiliated, but we've learned to work together since then."

Cara was relieved when Sheryl came over with a cardboard tray full of drinks. The picture of Lenae in dirty jeans was too damned appealing. She thanked Sheryl for the coffee and trailed behind the group as they walked the short distance back to the training center. She noticed every street crossing and obstacle Toby had led her past, amazed at how little awareness of her surroundings she'd had on the way there. Even without the blindfold, she let her other senses open like she should have while on the walk with Toby. Such a brief exercise, but her world seemed to have grown. She hoped she wouldn't forget the experience soon, reverting back to her flat way of seeing.

Once they had returned to the center, she and Lenae recorded a short discussion about the puppy walkers. Although Cara now had a better understanding of the gift they were offering the dogs and their new handlers, she still found it a sad prospect to love an animal only to let it go. She asked a few questions but let Lenae set the tone of the discussion without adding her belligerent opinion. She would have liked to visit with the puppies again, but George was signaling for her to hurry because the light was fading.

Cara spoke her closing remarks in front of the outdoor dog kennels, the most photogenic place on the property—mainly due to the animals in the runs, not the runs themselves. She hoped they wouldn't have to come back to reshoot any of the footage, like they had with the Baers. The segment was a sure hit, but Cara had felt too many conflicting emotions to be comfortable with the afternoon. She had felt out of her element and exposed during the walk with Toby. Unable to truly let go of control—not *wanting* to let go of control. The animals had saved the day. They were friendly and seemed to love people, a testament to Lenae's training methods, if not to her personality.

Lenae was an enigma. Unreadable and closed, with flashes of humor and personality. Cara wasn't sure what to make of her, except that she felt uncomfortable and off-kilter in Lenae's presence. She thought she'd be relieved to hit the road, to spin tall tales and joke about Lenae's scandalous ulterior motives when George asked for the *real* story, but instead, when he asked, she only said, "I don't know."

CHAPTER FIVE

Cara kept replaying the filming of Lenae's segment while she dressed for dinner. Lenae had seemed defensive and distant at times, but the dogs in her care were happy and full of life. Did she come to life once the cameras were off?

Cara added another layer of makeup to her face. From the Baer house to Lenae's to tonight before dinner, she had been gradually building on the foundation she had put on before she'd left her house that morning. She touched up her mascara, so her lashes de-emphasized tired green eyes, and put a new coat of lip gloss over the ones she had worn off while she talked all day. Pleated black slacks and a silky magenta shell replaced the more casual clothes she'd had on at Lenae's center.

She hadn't had a chance to find out about the real Lenae after the filming had finished. She hadn't wanted to stick around for her usual post-shooting chat, when masks were dropped and she was able to uncover the passion and personality of the subjects of her show. Instead, she had used tonight's obligation as an excuse to leave as soon as the main filming had finished.

She had considered bringing a date to tonight's monthly family dinner, but she had been disappointed too many times in the past. At first, she had been surprised each time she realized the woman she'd thought was a potential long-term girlfriend was merely an aspiring starlet hoping to be invited into the Bradleys' world. Later, she had tried not to care whether her dates were only interested in her looks or her name. But the superficial desires of those women, combined with the coldness of her family, had left her numb.

Worse than numb. She had been left wondering whether there really *was* more to her than the surface everyone seemed to see. She made her cynical jokes about the people she interviewed, felt the customary letdown of disbelief in true self-sacrifice and goodness, because she didn't have any proof that they existed in her own life. She observed them, yes, on a regular basis. But she had no idea what it would feel like to *live* them.

Lenae had been different somehow. There was something real about her. She was prickly and distant. Human. Not a Pollyanna, perfect-world kind of do-gooder that Cara couldn't imagine existing in real life, day after day, regardless of life's ups and downs. Lenae must have reasons for her defenses, although Cara wasn't going to find out what they were—nor did she want to.

Cara drove north from her home in Olympia, through heavy rush hour traffic in Seattle, to her parents' home on Mercer Island. The sun had set, and the lights from the Island's houses reflected off the choppy water of Lake Washington.

"Darling! Come in. You look adorable tonight." Lydia, her mother, greeted her with a kiss on each cheek. Cara wondered who else had been invited to eat with them, since her mom wouldn't welcome her so enthusiastically if no one outside the family was there.

"Come meet Talia. She's the new arts critic for the *Times*. She just moved to Seattle, so we wanted to welcome her to our beautiful city."

Ah, the kiss and welcome were explained. Cara said hello, but Talia seemed to have eyes only for Richard, Cara's brother. Cara sat on the love seat and watched the scene unfold as a spectator this time, not as a participant, while Richard leaned back in his chair, as regal as he was when playing a king in a Shakespearean play. He encouraged Talia's attention, bestowing his charming smiles on her and asking about her past. Cara knew his attention wouldn't survive beyond the night—he was content with his seemingly endless string of casual boyfriends—but tonight he acted as if Talia were the guest of honor at a royal banquet.

Cara loved her brother and admired his classically developed talent as an actor, but she saw the chasm of difference between them in the way they responded to flattery and starstruck adoration. Richard, like their parents, came alive with the attention. They were animated and kinder to one another than when they were in private. They sparkled with the very star quality that Talia wanted to see. Cara, on the other hand, withdrew inside herself even as she kept up the façade of the Bradley name. She had felt empty, hollow, when her name and family—instead of her true self—had been the center of a woman's attention, whether on dates or at parties and openings. Maybe her family recognized the shallowness of Talia's interest, but they seemed to thrive on it, believe they deserved it. Talia's kind of attention only made Cara grow less certain that there was anything deeper to see in any of the Bradleys, even herself.

"Your mother has some incredible news for you, Cara." Her father pulled her to the center of the conversation. She had been quite comfortable hanging out on the edges of it.

"Howard, you spoiled my big reveal." Lydia shook her head in Talia's direction, with the long-suffering but indulgent smile of a doting wife. Cara wanted to gag, and she had a feeling whatever news her mother had would make the reflex even worse. "I was waiting for the perfect time to tell her."

Cara took a drink of her scotch and soda. "Tell me what, Mother?"

Lydia put her hands together as if she was praying and pressed her index fingers against her lips for a moment—drawing out the suspense—before she spread her hands wide. "I got you a part on my sitcom."

"A…what?" Cara had been mesmerized by the gestures her mom was making, and wondering how many different movements she had practiced in a mirror before choosing this one, so she was caught off guard by the pronouncement.

"A part, dear. On my show." Lydia turned to Talia. "Did you know I act in a little sitcom? A darling show. I'm quite proud of it. I play the matriarch of a large family—I'm wealthy, and my children are all vying for my fortune. You'd play my maid, Cara. The part is small, but there are some quite funny moments. It would be great exposure for you, with a chance to be seen on television. Do stop gaping at me like that, dear."

Cara managed to close her mouth, but she struggled for words. Richard shrugged and sighed when she looked to him for support—he understood but wouldn't step in. "I'm already on television. Every week."

"Yes, of course you are." Howard leaned over and patted her on the knee. "But that's public television. This would be a nationally syndicated show. You'd be seen by millions instead of the handful of people who watch you grubbing through the mud."

"I wasn't…the segment was about a man who's restoring native plants to the prairie habitats in the region. I was helping him with some seedlings."

Howard and Lydia both gave similar waves of dismissal. Talia watched the family interchange with interest, and Cara figured she was wishing she had a pen and pad with her for taking notes. "Mother, I am *not* playing your maid on TV or anywhere else. I don't care how many people see my show. I do it because I like sharing stories about people who are doing good things for others and for the environment, not because I want my face on television."

Lydia gave a dramatic sniff. "I wish you knew how hard I worked to get this opportunity for you. Howard, talk some sense into your daughter."

"Really, Cara, why don't you do the show? If only to make your mother happy. You'll still have time to film your little program."

Cara deliberately set her drink on the table before she flung the glass against a wall. Despite her jokes and cynical repartee with George, she knew her program was getting people and organizations the funding and volunteers they so desperately needed. Her work was worthwhile. She grasped the memory of walking with Toby that afternoon. How important he would be to someone who was traveling through the world without sight. She had felt lost and isolated simply wearing a blindfold for a few minutes, and he had guided her safely. How much more meaningful would the experience be when his new owner picked up the harness and took those first steps with him? And now Cara had played a small part in sharing Lenae's story with the public.

"My *little show* helps people. Just today I interviewed a guide-dog trainer named Lenae McIntyre. She needs money for her center and people to volunteer as puppy walkers, and because her segment will be shown on my program, she'll have a chance to get what she needs."

"Lenae McIntyre?" Talia asked. "The newswriter for Three-N?"

"Yes. At least she was." Cara was aware of the sudden change in the room. Suddenly her show was interesting to these people, not just her target audience. "She left the network and runs her center full-time now."

"But she'll still have contacts in the industry, of course," Lydia said. "What's a puppy walker, Cara? It sounds adorable!"

At least her parents were no longer concerned with the role of the maid. Cara should have been relieved. Happy, even, since her family pestered her throughout dinner for information about the segment she had filmed at Lenae's, as if her work mattered to them. But she knew it didn't. She was aware their interest would only last as long as they thought the connection with Lenae might open some doors with Three-N or elsewhere. Even though they were asking about the show she had produced today, they seemed unable to grasp the reality of her experience. She had a feeling they were picturing her in the future—sitting in the anchor position and not walking to Starbucks with Toby.

CHAPTER SIX

Lenae set down the braille book she had been reading and walked into the kitchen. She shut off the beeping microwave and took out the leftover lasagna she had reheated. The smell of basil and garlic filled the air as she gathered a fork and napkin and carried her dinner to the dining-room table. She heard the click of toenails as Baxter came into the room and lay down at her feet, gnawing on the bone she had given him earlier that evening.

She ate with her left hand while her right skimmed the mystery novel she was reading. The day had been stressful, but worthwhile. Filming the television show, arguing with Cara, feeling the stress of everything that could have gone wrong. Cara's defensive attitude—admittedly matched by Lenae's own—had been short-lived, and they had been able to return to a professional level. Toby had behaved beautifully. Lenae wasn't sure what would happen during editing, but she hoped the center would get the positive publicity it needed.

Lenae went back to her fridge and got a can of parmesan cheese. She walked easily through the rooms in her suite above the center's office. She rarely had guests in her home, preferring to meet in restaurants when she got together with friends, because home was her sanctuary, the one place she could be certain no one would move objects or change anything. Her movement was free and unrestricted here, and she had been through the house so many times she no longer had to count paces. Here, Baxter was her companion and pet, not her guide, and she was as mobile as someone with sight.

She touched the edge of her plate to orient herself before pouring some cheese in her palm and sprinkling it on her food. She needed this haven tonight. She still had to find two more puppy walkers, and the center seemed to be perpetually in debt. Even though she wanted to ignore the disrepair she couldn't see, Des had been nagging her to get the grounds in better shape. She hated spending money on anything besides her dogs, but the first impressions people got when they came to the center mattered more than she wanted to admit. Plus, she had overheard an embarrassing debate between George and Sheryl over which camera angles would best hide the weedy lawn and unpainted fencing. Her five-year plan to make the training program a success had to include some cosmetic improvements.

She didn't worry too much about how her place would come across on the screen, though. She had formed her own opinions about what Cara looked like based on her voice, and she doubted anyone would notice much beyond Cara's beauty when she was in the shot. Des had made some comments about Cara's appearance in response to Lenae's casual questioning, and she had learned that Cara had blond hair with reddish highlights, green eyes, and was very slender. The actual details didn't mean much to Lenae, but the associations helped her form an idea of Cara. Her hair had some of the same tones people had mentioned when talking about Baxter's coat. Green for her eyes brought to mind the fir trees so prevalent in the Northwest, with their soft and waxy needles and resiny-sweet scent. Lenae had been able to determine Cara's size based on her voice and the delicate bones of her wrist. Their contact had been brief, but having touched her, Lenae would be able to identify the texture and feel of Cara's skin from among hundreds of people.

It was rare for her to have such a strong impression of another person after a brief meeting. There'd be vague associations—

usually words like names or occupations—but she felt as if she'd recognize Cara immediately by touch, by the scent of oranges and cream, by the liquid of her voice…

"We'll have to assume I'm right," she said to Baxter. He sat up and rested his head on her thigh. She picked a chunk of mozzarella from her lasagna and fed it to him. "Because I'm never going to have a chance to test my hypothesis."

❖

"I wrote a list of the improvements we need to make around here," Des said at their next morning meeting. "Yesterday during the filming, I looked at this place differently, like someone who was showing up for the first time. We need to fix it up."

Lenae had been dwelling on the prior day's events as well—namely on distracting thoughts of Cara. What she needed was to put her mind on the dogs and the future of her center, not on the television crew's visit. She ran her fingertips quickly over the list Des had converted to braille.

"Reseed the lawn? Repair the fence around the obstacle course? Paint the house?" She held the paper in front of her and he took it out of her hand. "All of those things take money and time we just don't have. Most of the people coming here will be—"

"I know, I know. Our clients will be vision impaired and will be more interested in meeting their dogs than caring about the lawn or the house. But we'll have other visitors, too. People who want to donate time or money. Representatives from corporations offering grants. If they see this place in disrepair, it might affect their decisions."

"Maybe they'll decide that we desperately need their money." Lenae heard the grumbling in her voice. She felt grouchy, but didn't need to take it out on Des. He wasn't the one who had given her a sleepless night. Cara, who probably knew all too well that looks were the secret to success, had been the one consuming her thoughts. "You're right. Much as I dislike the idea, improving the way the center looks will have to be a priority. But it's not our top priority. We'll just have to do those projects as we can, over the next year. Now, let's talk about the dogs."

"Toby did awesome yesterday." Des couldn't keep the excitement out of his voice. Lenae felt the same. The dog had been wonderful, even with an inexperienced handler. He had followed direction well but had taken the initiative when he had needed to protect Cara. "He and the other two are ready for next week. I can't wait until we pair them with their new owners."

"There's nothing like it," Lenae said. She had been present for meetings between anxious new handlers and guide dogs before, but Des hadn't. "Be prepared for an overload of emotions. Most will be joyous and excited, but there will also be fear. Even anger because the person doesn't want to face the need for guidance and help. But bear with it because after a week or so, everything will settle. What about the dogs entering the program? What's your evaluation of them?"

Des hesitated. "They're good. They all seem to have the right attitude, so hopefully they'll take well to the harness training."

"Hmm. Okay. So, what's on your mind?"

"How do you always know?"

Lenae laughed. "You never pause before speaking your mind unless you have something challenging to say."

"I'll have to watch out for that." Des echoed her laugh. "But you're right. I've been thinking about Gem. Maybe, if she does well in training, we should keep her at the center. She'd have some great puppies, I'll bet."

Gem. Lenae easily called to mind the sensitive young Lab. She was one of the new animals, fresh out of the puppy-walking experience, ready to begin the serious work of being a guide dog. She'd make someone a loving partner, but with her good breeding and excellent temperament, she'd be an asset as a breeding dog as well. Lenae hated pulling a promising animal out of the program, but she had to keep an eye on long-term goals.

"What are your reasons?" she asked.

"She has nice conformation and she's easy to work with. Most of the larger training centers are breeding their own puppies, and it would mean fewer dogs we'd need to purchase over the long run, even if we only breed her every other year or so."

"And?" Lenae prompted. She understood the logistics, but she wanted to hear the sentiment behind the suggestion.

Des was silent for a moment. "We've bonded pretty strongly. I love all the dogs, of course, but she's something special. I thought she could live with me, and I'd take care of the pups until they're ready to go to new homes. I'd reimburse the center for her, and—"

Lenae waved to stop his rushed sentences. "You're right. She'd be a wonderful mother, and in the long run it'll be good for the center. No money—this is a gift from me to both of you. Put her through the basic training first, just to make sure she's well suited for the work. I wouldn't want to breed her right away, but I was thinking of doing some guide dog demos for schools and community events. The two of you might be able to work up a little routine, and she could be a mascot of sorts for the center."

"I'm going to hug you now," Des warned her.

Lenae sighed with mock exasperation. "Go ahead, but make it quick."

Des gave her an awkward hug and then said he needed to check on the dogs. Lenae figured he was going out to tell Gem the news, so she stayed in the office and let him have his time alone in the kennels. Short-term sacrifices for long-term good.

She picked up the list of repairs Des had made and moved through it more slowly this time. Her phone chimed while she was contemplating the item *plant flowers near the office*. She loved flowers for their beautiful aromas and velvety soft petals, but landscaping the property would be expensive and time-consuming to maintain. She tossed the list on the desk and answered her cell. "Hello."

"Lenae McIntyre?"

She didn't recognize the voice. "Yes."

"This is Howard Bradley, sportscaster for Channel 7."

Lenae was silent for a moment while she tried to recall whether the name meant anything to her. She came up blank.

"You met my daughter yesterday. Cara Bradley."

Now that was a voice Lenae knew all too well. "She filmed a segment for her show here, yes. How can I help you?"

"Not me, but her. The publicity from her little program will help your center, so I thought you might be willing to return the favor."

Of course. Lenae should have known that any media exposure would come with a price. What the hell did Cara want? Lenae wasn't in the business anymore. Of course she could introduce Cara to the right people at Three-N, but she would rather have suggested it herself, not be coerced into doing it. She hated feeling used.

"What does she want?"

"My station is willing to let her have a regular weekly spot on the evening news. Last night at dinner, she told us about the puppy-walking program and it seems perfect for her. People love puppies. She could have one of the dogs and update the audience on her progress training it every—"

"No."

"But you'd have your center on the news every week. Seen by thousands of people."

"No." Lenae wasn't going to budge. Give one of her puppies to a media flake who was only interested in her own advancement? If this had been Cara's plan from the start, why had she seemed so bitter during the discussion about puppy walkers and their willingness to let go of the animals that had spent a year with them?

"Maybe I should mention that my family's foundation is planning to offer a sizable grant to a local nonprofit. Since we just started the program this year, we don't have a pool of applicants, so I thought we'd offer the initial grant to your center. Based on the recommendation of Cara, of course."

Of course. "Mr. Bradley, I appreciate the offer, but—"

"Did I forget to mention the amount of the grant?"

He told her the sum, and Lenae found herself hesitating. It wasn't as if Cara would be mean to the puppy, it was just that she'd be in the program for the wrong reasons. Besides, with that money she and Des could buy a lot of flowers and fence paint and dogs and kennels and...

"Thank you, but no. We do serious training here, and puppy-walking spots are not for sale. Good-bye, Mr. Bradley."

Lenae disconnected before she could be further tempted. The money would have been helpful, but the price was far too high.

CHAPTER SEVEN

Cara parked her Camry in front of Lenae's office. The center seemed to have grown dingier overnight, as if it had done its best to impress the cameras and now collapsed back to its original state. She got out of her car, noticing that her vehicle didn't do much to spruce up the place. It looked as neglected as its surroundings.

A chorus of barks greeted her as she walked past the gate leading to the backyard. She wanted to detour for a visit to the runs, but she needed to face Lenae sooner rather than later. The door wasn't fully closed, and it swung open when she knocked on it. She stood in the entryway listening to the sound of a cranked-up radio playing oldies and the voice of someone singing along with Carl Carlton. Lenae. Off-key and loud, in a charming and total shift from the put-together role she had been playing yesterday. Cara looked down the long hallway, trying to locate the source of the music.

"Hello? Lenae, are you here?" Baxter rounded the corner with a clatter of nails on hardwood and ran to her, waving his tail in greeting. Cara crouched to pet him. "Hey, Baxter. Where's your mom?"

He trotted back the way he had come, and Cara sashayed after him, humming along with the music, until they came to a room outfitted as an office. A large desk was covered with tidy piles of envelopes and invoices. A computer and printer sat on folding tables along the far wall. Spartan and functional, except for the floor with its large plaid dog bed and pile of chew toys and fuzzy animals. Lenae sat in a black leather office chair with a small gray machine in front of her and a Bose radio within reach.

Cara's humming had progressed to singing along at the top of her voice, and she found herself shouting into the silence as Lenae abruptly turned off the radio. "Oops, sorry. I didn't mean to interrupt, but that's one of my favorite songs."

"Mine, too," Lenae said after a brief hesitation. Her hand hovered over the radio's buttons, and Cara hoped she was about to turn the music on again so they could finish their duet. But Lenae pushed the Bose to one side of her desk and rested her fingers on the other machine. "I didn't expect you today, Cara. I already told your father I wasn't interested in your proposal."

Cara sighed. She had come here immediately after her dad had called with his brilliantly annoying plan, and she had hoped to have a chance to explain how her family meddled before Lenae spoke to him. Obviously, judging by the cranky note in Lenae's voice, she was too late for that.

"It wasn't my idea. I came to apologize for him."

Lenae shook her head, but she waved in the general area of the second office chair. "I need to finish converting this application while it's fresh in my mind. If you don't mind waiting, we can talk in a few minutes."

"Sure. I have time." Cara didn't go over to the chair but instead moved closer to Lenae's desk, watching over her shoulder as she typed information on the machine in front of her. There were only nine different keys, and Lenae's fingers flew with clearly practiced skill. A sheet of paper emerged, blank at first glance, but Cara could see the small shadows made by the raised dots.

"Here. You can feel it if you want." Lenae handed Cara the sheet of paper. Even though she had been silent, Lenae seemed to know exactly where she was standing. Cara ran her fingers over the bumps and tried to detect patterns while part of her wondered what else Lenae might invite her to feel if she showed an interest. The thought was intriguing, but she had to focus on her purpose for coming here.

"Thank you," she said, handing the paper back to Lenae. "It doesn't seem possible that there are discernible words and sentences there when all I feel is a series of dots. Was it difficult to learn braille?"

As soon as the words came out, Cara regretted them. She remembered how she had felt when Sheryl and George praised Toby after their walk to Starbucks, making her feel like an object to be guided along. She hoped she hadn't insulted Lenae by acting surprised that she could learn. "That was a silly question, wasn't it? I learned to read as a child, so why would it have been any different for you to learn a different format?"

Lenae turned off her Brailler and felt for the stack of applications from hopeful candidates who wanted guide dogs. She put the newest form on top of the pile while she processed Cara's comments. Frankness, respect. Two things Lenae didn't encounter often. From Cara's loud musical entrance this morning to her thoughtful and self-reflective words, Lenae was finding it more difficult to maintain the anger she had felt after Howard Bradley's call. "I don't mind the question. Braille is subtler than written letters, I think. For someone who isn't accustomed to using their fingers to differentiate such tiny details, it can seem too challenging to learn, but it's all I've known, so it was easy for me." Lenae cleared her throat, caught unaware by the desire to show Cara just how sensitive her fingers could be. Definitely not the right direction for the conversation to go, so she changed to a less personal example. "Des has picked it up quickly since he came to work for me, although he's studied several languages and might have an advantage there."

"I took French in school," Cara said. "Maybe you could teach me a little?"

Lenae didn't answer right away. The thought of guiding Cara's hand was tempting, but she had to keep focused on her center, not on the scent and sensation of Cara who was leaning against her desk. Too close. Lenae put distance between them with her words and the cold tone she heard in her own voice. "I'm pretty busy right now, training people who want to help with the center, not people who want to use my puppies to advance their careers."

Lenae felt Cara shift away from her. The energy Lenae had felt when Cara was close dissipated, and Lenae wished she hadn't sounded so harsh. She had to protect her center—and herself—from self-serving people. But despite first impressions, and her father's phone call, Lenae wasn't entirely convinced Cara was one of the bad guys.

"I didn't know what he was planning to do," Cara said. "Last night we had a family dinner, and I talked about the segment we'd filmed. That was all. As soon as he called this morning, I came over here to say I was sorry."

"To say you're sorry?" Lenae repeated. She hadn't expected Cara to say those words, in a voice tinged with something indefinable. Embarrassment? Anger? She'd expected sweet pleas and empty promises. "For what?"

"I don't want to do a weekly spot on the network news." Cara stopped just short of petulance, but she sounded somehow childlike as she spoke. Not childish, but helpless. "I don't want to be responsible for raising a puppy that will be doing such important work. I just want to do my public television show and teach a few classes. No one seems to understand that."

Lenae hesitated. Was this some sort of reverse-psychology ploy? Cara sounded truthful, but Lenae had no way of detecting honesty. She used to think she was a good judge of character, but she'd been proven wrong. She wanted to believe the happy-go-lucky Cara who had burst into her office was the real one, but Lenae had let personal desires cloud her common sense before.

"It's a huge commitment." *I'm sure you'd do fine. The animals love you.* She wanted to reassure Cara for some inexplicable reason. But the truth was that Cara had no business puppy walking if she was only doing it for herself and for the attention she'd gain. Lenae had no choice but to agree with Cara's alleged disinclination to volunteer. "There are weekly classes, and you're expected to take the puppy almost everywhere you go since they need to be exposed to stores and public transportation. And although the center covers vet bills, there are the daily financial responsibilities as well. You can't just take the puppy out when the cameras are on."

"Right. I know all that." Cara's throat felt tight, and she had trouble forcing the words out. She didn't have the time or desire to take on a puppy, but Lenae didn't need to imply that Cara was unable to do the necessary work. Cara had factored in all those considerations when she'd decided to reject the proposal. Didn't that make her more responsible, not less? She didn't have time to commit to puppy walking, didn't want to acquiesce to her dad's interference. But, perversely, she also didn't want Lenae to think she wasn't capable or trustworthy. The first two were reasonable excuses for not volunteering. The third had nothing to do with logic, but everything to do with her inexplicable reaction to Lenae. "I understand the requirements involved. But maybe I couldn't love an animal for a year and then give it away."

Lenae shrugged. "Not everyone can. There are different kinds of love in the world, and it takes a certain kind to make a good puppy walker. It's best for the center and for the animals if you acknowledge your feelings now instead of at the end of the program."

Cara tapped her fingers absently on a pile of papers in front of her. They slid across the table, and she picked them up to get them back in order. Some papers were in braille, some in print. Bills from the vet, a mortgage statement. Cara put the papers back on the desk in a neat stack. She had originally started her show as a way to give back to her community, to encourage volunteerism, to raise awareness of the people and organizations doing good work. Was she such a hypocrite that she wasn't willing to do the work she asked others to do, week after week? She spent a few hours a month smiling at the camera, and then she went back to her own world, confident that she'd done her part to save the world. Maybe Lenae was right in her assessment. Maybe Cara was shallower than she cared to admit.

"It's not that I *couldn't* do it. I just realize how hard it would be."

"Right. There are always lots of tears when the dogs are returned to the center. But there's joy, as well. Hope."

Hope. Cara had been searching for it but had never seemed to find it. "Dad said he offered you a big grant."

Lenae felt her face tighten in a frown and she relaxed the muscles. The figure Howard Bradley had quoted kept dancing through her mind. "Yes, he did."

"And the money would be helpful for your center?"

"Yes, but not if it means one of our puppies doesn't receive the proper training. Money is always in short supply for a nonprofit, but I'm not in a hurry to make this place a success. I have a long-term plan, and while the grant money would help us move more quickly through the initial stages, I'm not going to sacrifice the quality of work we're doing just to get ahead."

"Jeez, it's not like I'm Cruella De Vil offering to puppy walk all the black-and-white dogs."

Lenae had to laugh at Cara's injured tone. "I know you're not a bad person. But I also know that you're not interested in any part of the puppy-walking experience. Except the fun, showy parts."

"Do you really think I'd be a detriment to your program? That I'd willingly neglect a puppy?"

"Not at all." Lenae wasn't certain when the conversation had shifted from them agreeing Cara wasn't a good match to Cara arguing for a chance to volunteer. "But you said you didn't want to do this." One thing was certain—Cara confused her.

"I said I didn't want to be pushed into something just because my father thinks it's a good career move. And I didn't want to volunteer just so I could be on television doing it. But did you ever think I might be interested in helping just because I like dogs and think it'd be fun to be a puppy walker?"

"No," Lenae said. "Because you just said—"

"You want to volunteer as a puppy walker?" Des entered the room and caught only the end of the conversation. "Cool! You were great with Toby, and we really need a couple more volunteers, don't we, Lenae? I'll go pick one out for you."

"Um…" Cara wasn't sure how she had managed to talk her way into this mess. She had been angry at the accusation that she wasn't capable of handling the responsibility of a puppy, but she wanted to prove she was responsible through words, not necessarily through a year of her time. Chewed-up shoes, puppy classes, and forced news segments. No way.

But there was a stack of bills on the desk. No matter how much Lenae might talk about her long-term, patient plan to establish the center, she would need money to get her through. Cara had seen the temptation in Lenae's tired frown when they had talked about the grant. And with the property in such a run-down state, there'd be more than dog food to buy before all the repairs could be made. The grant, plus the regular network news spot, might be the difference between the center surviving its first few years, or having to close its doors permanently.

The final argument for Cara came bursting through the door in a flurry of brown fur and white paws. She slid out of her chair and onto the floor as Pickwick hurled himself into her arms.

"I'll do it," she said to Lenae as her face was bathed in doggy kisses.

CHAPTER EIGHT

Cara ran through her house, tossing articles of clothing over her shoulder and dumping them in whatever closet she reached first. She stacked books and loose papers along the walls of her living room and shoved an armload of expensive film gear into the pantry, silently praying that nothing had broken in the process and that none of her hastily formed stacks would collapse. She did a quick walk-through from her front door to the living room and into the guest bathroom, to be certain nothing would be in the way of Lenae and Baxter's path as they moved around her house. She moved her coffee table closer to the couch—within easy reach for Lenae—and shoved her old recliner away a few feet to make a path wide enough for a person and a large retriever walking side-by-side.

Once she was finished with her haphazard cleaning, she collapsed on her chair for a few minutes' rest before Lenae arrived. She didn't even have approval for getting a puppy yet, and she was already feeling the strain of yet another obligation. Her morning had been filled with meetings—a production meeting for her show and a staff meeting for her seminar at Evergreen. Both had required hours of preparation and had resulted in more hours of work to be done. She simply didn't have time to have Lenae scrutinizing her life and home. She had let her emotions get in the way of sound decision-making, succumbing to Pickwick's charms and the foolish desire to impress Lenae. Now her life was going to be turned upside down—pending Lenae's approval, of course—and her dad would believe she should be indebted to him for advancing her career.

Although she had spontaneously volunteered to puppy walk, Lenae hadn't been easy to convince. She had insisted Cara go through the whole process, from application to home visit, before they could go forward with the project. Cara didn't mind the formality of the procedure—after all, her decision had been more about Lenae's center and Pickwick than about the news segment—but she had a feeling Lenae would be even more vigilant with her than with a normal applicant. Cara was used to people assuming she was as two-dimensional as her television persona, but she still resented it.

"Yuk," Cara said as she pulled herself out of the comfortable chair when she heard a knock on the door. Home was private. A place where she could be herself, with no cameras or need to perform. Now her dad's expectations for her career and Lenae's stringent requirements for the role of puppy walker were invading her space. She opened the door, expecting to need all her acting skills to get through the interview, but her genuine pleasure at the sight of Lenae and Baxter was almost as disturbing as her dread of the visit had been.

"Hi, Lenae," she said, stepping back and holding the door wide open. "Hey, Baxter. Come on in. Let me take your jacket, Lenae. Can I get you some coffee?"

Cara paused in her chattering long enough to inhale deeply as she hung Lenae's coat near the door. Chanel and the dusty smell of fresh rain. A few gold hairs clung to the denim, and Cara hoped they belonged to Baxter and not some other woman. None of her business. She cleared her throat and led Baxter and Lenae into her living room.

"Coffee would be nice, thank you," Lenae said. She sat on the couch and Baxter immediately lay down over her feet. "It's chillier than I expected today."

Cara poured two mugs and brought them into the room. She took part in the idle chitchat about the drizzly weather and how Lenae took her coffee—black and sweet—while most of her thoughts were concentrated on the unfamiliar experience of having guests in her home. She had been paying attention to the visual aspects of her house during her frantic cleanup just prior to Lenae's visit, but now she felt her senses expand. She heard the background whirr of the heater and the occasional car outside. The smell of damp dog combined with coffee and Lenae's subtle perfume somehow warmed her house more than the heater did. Cara itched to slide her hands over Lenae's jeans, the same rough denim as her jacket, and over the silky material of her gray shirt. Cara's world seemed to broaden when she was around Lenae.

"This is a quiet neighborhood," Lenae said.

Quiet was relative. Cara heard every creak inside the house and every movement on the street outside. "The street is safe for kids and pets, plus I have a fenced yard. It's tiny, but puppy proof."

Lenae felt for the table in front of her. Cara had placed a coaster within easy reach, and Lenae set her mug on it. She didn't like going into other people's unfamiliar homes where she was out of her element and exposed if anything had been carelessly left in her way, but she had discovered how important it was to get a sense of the homes where her puppies and dogs would live. No matter how much a person cleaned, they couldn't erase the atmosphere of their house. Lenae might not trust her instincts in most situations anymore, but she was confident in her ability to feel a household's kindness or lack of it.

"Can you give me a tour?" she asked. Normally she'd stay put when on a home visit, but she was interested in getting to know the rest of Cara's home. For reasons entirely too personal for comfort. Cara was an enigma. Lenae had formed assumptions about her, based on her reported looks and her career, but the house didn't support them. Lenae felt its coldness...no, not coldness. Emptiness. She had been expecting to sense the echoed memory of wild parties, but Cara seemed almost nervous, as if she was unaccustomed to having visitors.

"Of course."

Lenae stood up. She heard a clunk—Cara's mug hitting the table?—and the rustling sounds of her getting out of her seat, and she expected Cara to grab her arm like most people did in similar situations.

"Right this way," Cara said instead, moving away from Lenae and letting Baxter do his job. Lenae followed with relief.

"This is the guest bathroom. It's tastefully furnished in blues and greens, with a seashell motif. Thanks to my mother who apparently didn't approve of the roll of paper towels I had in there instead of guest towels when she first visited. And down here is a spare room that I use as an office. You and Baxter are free to explore in there if you want, but I might have to send a search party in to find you. The floor is covered with old textbooks and cameras."

"We'll just appreciate it from the doorway." Lenae laughed as Baxter stood in front of her legs as if blocking her way into the room. "Baxter doesn't want me to go in."

"Smart dog," Cara said. "He knows his limitations. I haven't ventured in there since last semester. I'll keep this door closed if Pickwick comes here."

"Good idea," Lenae agreed. She had been determined to fully vet Cara before she gave her a puppy, but she could already imagine him there with Cara. Crowding out the loneliness she sensed within the walls.

"Now we'll go back through the living room," Cara said. Baxter eagerly followed her on the short walk to the now-familiar room. "Please keep your arms and legs on the path at all times. I cleared enough space for you and Baxter to walk, but that means everything from the floor is now piled along the walls."

Lenae tentatively put her hand out to her side and felt an uneven and wobbly stack of thick books. She heard Cara's snort of laughter.

"Were you always this way? If someone says *Don't touch that*, do you have to touch it? You must have been a handful for your parents."

Lenae smiled. "I'm too curious for my own good, sometimes." Her mother had never wanted her to feel she was at a disadvantage, but even so, Lenae knew she had tried her mom's patience with her relentless need to be independent. She was here to learn about Cara, though, not to talk about herself. Unfortunately, she liked what she was learning, far too much. Cara could easily have lied and said her house was perfectly cleaned and organized, but she was willing to laugh at herself and admit to the truth.

Lenae wanted to linger when they came to Cara's bedroom. She wanted to ask about the color scheme and to feel the sheets and pillows that Cara slept on each night. She was getting too involved for her own good, and she needed to distance herself from the growing attraction she felt to Cara—not just to the tangible qualities of voice and scent and energy, but now to her polite respect for Lenae's space, her honesty, and her self-deprecating humor.

Once they were back in the living room, Lenae pulled out a packet of information from her bag. "Let's talk about your responsibilities now," she said, giving up all pretense of screening Cara and burying her own reaction to the home visit under a load of detailed and objective information. She managed to talk without pause, and without emotion, engulfing them both in a cloud of data until it was time for her and Baxter to go.

Cara dropped into her recliner again after Lenae left. She raised the footrest and settled back in the chair, trying to ignore the pages strewn across her coffee table, full of information about feeding Pickwick and cleaning his ears and trimming his nails. She was surprised Lenae hadn't explained how to dial the phone in case of an emergency. But she seemed to have passed the test since Lenae had set a time for Des to come and inspect her house before Pickwick was delivered to her. She jabbed at the stack of information with her foot. This new job was going to be a lot of work, but she had liked having a dog around the house today.

She had liked having Lenae here, too, when she was smiling and friendly. But just like before, as quickly as flipping off a radio, Lenae had changed from friendly and open to detached and severely businesslike. Cara had a feeling the first was the real person, but she couldn't get that Lenae to settle down and stay for long. Cara smiled. She wanted the poised Lenae to break into out-of-tune singing again. She had a year ahead with Lenae and Pickwick—maybe she'd get to hear another song.

CHAPTER NINE

Cara turned off Highway 101 and wound through the tall firs on her way to Evergreen State College. Pickwick sat next to her on the passenger seat and gnawed on the seat-belt buckle. Cara gently pushed his nose away and offered him a chew toy instead, but before she could get her hand back on the steering wheel, he was back to work on the plastic buckle. Cara sighed and added *How to stop him from chewing on inappropriate items?* to her growing list of questions for her first puppy-walking class with Lenae. She had been told the basics—teach general good manners and commands like sit and stay—but she wasn't sure how to instill positive habits in Pickwick or, more importantly, how to discourage the negative ones.

At least Pickwick had been welcomed at the college without hesitation. Although Cara had followed a formal educational path, from a double major in communications and drama at the University of Washington to her graduate degree from Columbia, she reveled in the nontraditional collaborative and interdisciplinary approach at Evergreen. Students were encouraged to design their own curriculum, drawing on diverse fields of study, and most classes were team taught. This term, Cara was leading a seminar called Rooted in Place. Along with professors from the media arts, sociology, and cultural studies departments, she had planned a course of study that explored cultural and familial roots and influences. The class would culminate in a student-made film about the particular stories of each person in the seminar. This was the first course she had created—from inception to reading list to syllabus—and she was anxious to meet her students and get started on the project she had been planning for months.

Cara waggled the chew toy at Pickwick again, hoping to deter him from the buckle, but he wasn't interested in the squeaky duck. She tossed it in the backseat as she drove to the lower parking lot and stopped in a corner spot. She wasn't sure whether having Pickwick along and facing the certain excitement he'd bring to the class would help on her first day as team leader or not, but he would be her partner for the next year or more. Everywhere she went, he would go.

How the hell had she ended up puppy walking? Did she really volunteer for something so important merely in a knee-jerk reaction to Lenae's assumptions about her? Her entire response to Lenae, from the physical to the emotional, was complex.

She sighed. At least Des had been helpful. He had crawled around the floor of her small house, claiming he was trying to get a puppy's-eye view of the place. He had pointed out everything Pickwick might chew on or grab or mangle. Cara had thought he was being overly paranoid until she accidentally left her two-hundred-dollar running shoes on the floor of her bedroom. Pickwick had made sure they would never run again, and Cara had learned not to leave anything in what Des had called puppy space, until Pickwick was older.

Cara snapped the leash on Pickwick's collar, straightened his navy blue guide-dog-in-training cape, and got out of the car. Luckily, he wasn't supposed to walk at heel since he'd eventually be expected to walk in front of his handler. Cara didn't think she'd ever have been able to teach him to heel. He darted from bush to tree to person, often tangling her in his leash as he zigged and zagged. He greeted everyone, whether they looked like a dog person or not, and he seemed able to win over the crankiest people. Cara now automatically added an extra half-hour to every outing since she had to stop frequently to answer questions about

Pickwick or to wait while he was adored by his numerous fans. It was bound to get worse once they started filming the news segments, and the pair of them became recognizable.

Cara made her way across campus at Pickwick speed. For as much as the pup ran and darted around, he didn't make much forward progress at all. She had brought him with her once before, when she had needed to find a reference book in the library, and he seemed to love the campus as much as she did. It was dog friendly, with plenty of grassy spaces and greenery. The college seemed to be growing out of the forest around it. On her first visit, Cara had thought the stark buildings out of place, with their plain gray-and-red concrete and sharp angles. Less organic than the natural wood and softer shapes she had expected. But the low-lying squares and rectangles, molded as if part of the earth and hiding among ferns and fallen oak trees, soon grew on her. They were something ancient and modern at the same time. A hidden civilization, with innovative attitudes.

Cara waited while Pickwick peed on an industrial-looking metal sculpture, then led him into the communications building. He trotted along the rust-colored carpet, stopping to sniff something every few yards, only to return to her side and look up at her with his tongue lolling out of his mouth and a happy expression on his face. She couldn't help but smile back at him. The first few days of puppy guardianship had been hectic and overwhelming as she'd figured out how to coexist with a dog that seemed at least half beaver. She had been annoyed by her dad's smug attitude as he congratulated himself on talking her and Lenae into following his scheme. But Cara could admit the truth: her motivation had nothing to do with her own publicity and everything to do with a desire to promote Lenae's center. And, okay, she was irritated by Lenae's insinuation that she didn't have the integrity needed to do the job well.

But aside from all the vexations, she had already grown accustomed to Pickwick's presence in her life. She had woken up with a start the first evening when Pickwick jumped on her bed. Instead of insisting he go back to the soft cushion she had placed on the floor by her bedside, she had let him spin in a circle a few times before he curled in a ball at her side. The rhythm of puppy snores had soothed her into a deep sleep. The house was warmer with another being inside it. Pickwick didn't care how she looked or who her family was—he just seemed to adore her without reservation or ulterior motive.

Cara spent some time Pickwick proofing her office before she gathered her notes and books and set off down the hallway to one of the small seminar rooms. When she had last checked, twelve students had signed up for the course. She got to her assigned room fifteen minutes early, and she settled Pickwick on his favorite blanket with some food and water before she opened her briefcase and pulled out her notes and syllabi.

The students filed in soon after. They noticed Pickwick immediately, of course, since he insisted on greeting each one, but Cara waited until the entire class had assembled before she explained why he was in class with her.

"Welcome to Rooted in Place," she said as she handed a syllabus and reading list to each student. She had hoped to see a familiar face or two in the room, but she hadn't had any of these kids in previous classes. "I'm Cara Bradley, but more important, this is Pickwick. I'm puppy walking him for the McIntyre Training Center, and he'll be with me for the next year or more. If any of you have questions about the program, I'm glad to either answer them or refer you to Lenae McIntyre. She's always looking for willing volunteers."

Cara said the last sentence with a creepy expression, while rubbing her hands together as if Lenae was really looking for victims, not volunteers. She got the laugh she wanted from the gesture, and the subsequent relaxation in her presence. A few of the students asked about the guide-dog training and she answered as well as she could, given her limited experience.

"I have my first puppy-walking class tomorrow night because I need training even more than Pickwick does. I'll share what I learn with you each week. Any more questions about guide dogs before we start class?"

One student raised her hand and, at Cara's nod, asked, "It'd be fun to help, but I couldn't commit to a whole year of volunteering since I graduate soon. Is there anything I can do while I'm still here?"

Cara ran quickly through the alphabet before she remembered the girl's name. "I appreciate the offer, Nancy. I'm sure there'd be a way for you to help the center, but I'll check with Lenae to get some suggestions."

Another question on her growing list of them. Cara had conflicting feelings about seeing Lenae again. Lenae was attractive, but there was more appeal to her than looks. She was intelligent and dedicated, but she seemed to assume Cara was neither of those things. Cara didn't need to prove herself to anyone, so why did she care what Lenae thought of her? At least Pickwick gave her a way to be around Lenae without getting too personal, and without examining her own feelings too much. She'd have her hands full with his training and with all the information she needed to get from Lenae. Cara picked up Pickwick, who had jumped into her chair, and took her fountain pen out of his mouth before setting him on the floor and starting class.

"What does it mean to have roots in a geographic location, in a culture, an ethnicity, or a specific family? To what extent are we bound by those roots? Are we ever completely free to choose our own destiny, or do we create a future that branches out from—but always connects to—the past? We're going to approach these questions from a variety of angles—sociological, biological, and anthropological. We'll also explore how we can communicate our specific stories to others, through words and through images, as we produce a short film that will be shown to family and friends at the end of the term."

Cara went through the class syllabus with them, breaking down into week-by-week assignments the questions that had haunted her since childhood. How was she defined by her family and the values they embraced? Was she destined to be only a pretty face? Always seen by others as an image to be manipulated and not a real person worthy of love? Even though her television work accomplished meaningful goals, she sometimes felt like a mere conduit for emotions. She found people who did good work and mirrored their accomplishments with her expression and words during filming. She connected the doers with her audience members, but she never took part in the process beyond screen time. She was a channel, not a participant in life. The question of her own worth plagued her, reinforced by the complete lack of any such self-reflection by her parents. She might ponder these ideas, but the bare act of ruminating on them didn't make her any more substantial than they were.

Once they'd reviewed the syllabus, Cara invited her students to share some of their initial answers to her questions in relation to their unique histories. She half listened and half watched as Pickwick made the rounds of the classroom. He'd paw at each student in turn, dropping into play posture as he attempted to distract them from their studies. Cara considered calling him back to her side and ordering him to stay put, but she didn't want her class to see how little she was in control of him. If he ignored her completely, she'd lose face as an authority figure. Luckily, he returned to his blanket and started gnawing on the leg of her chair. Unpredictable, untrained, and determined to dismantle everything in his path. Still, he was the first physical manifestation in her own life of the kind of work she extolled on her show. She wasn't sure she'd survive the process, but he gave her life meaning in his silly puppy way, letting her share in Lenae's work for a brief time. Her sigh echoed his when he finally stopped his chewing and closed his eyes for a nap.

CHAPTER TEN

L et's go to the bistro, Baxter." Lenae had been roaming the streets for almost an hour, doing small errands and worrying about the meeting ahead. She had left the training center with plenty of time to spare but was now dragging her feet and running behind schedule. Baxter—always aware of her anxious moments—had led her from store to store, pressing his wet nose against her hand every time they paused. Lenae needed his reassuring presence. When she had first started making plans to open her center, she had been full of confidence and ambition. Set goals and achieve them. Develop a business plan and follow through with no deviation. She'd anticipated possible setbacks and challenges, but she hadn't expected emotions to be so involved with the work she did. She had merely wanted a quiet life spent working with the dogs she loved and trusted, but her new career had been anything but predictable and steady so far. How could she handle intense and troubled clients when she was fighting her own growing—and frightening—attraction to Cara?

She pushed through the door of Hoffmann's Bakery and Bistro and felt the raised dial of her watch. Five minutes late. She was never late for appointments. She didn't need to ask the hostess if Gene and Toby had arrived already because she felt Baxter's sniff of recognition and the increased energy of his wagging tail.

"Find Toby." She followed him on a zigzag course, presumably around tables full of other diners, although he made certain she never bumped into another person or tripped over a purse lying on the floor. He stopped, and she reached out for the chair she knew would be within easy reach.

"Hello, Gene." She sat down and oriented herself with the table setting, moving her plate and glass an inch to the right before she rested one hand on her lap and the other on Baxter's head. "I'm sorry I'm late. Did you find this place without trouble?"

"I've been here before," Gene said, his voice defensive as usual.

"I know you have. But it's different now," Lenae said, her tone soothing as she attempted to reach this man who had so much anger inside. She recognized in his voice the same tone she had used with Cara at her house, when she'd felt the intimacy of walking through Cara's rooms too keenly. Distant, rejecting closeness. Grasping for control. After her initial consultations, she had been confident in her decision to pair him with the gentle and happy Toby, but she had never worked with a handler who had been sighted since birth and had recently lost his vision, and she had underestimated the helpless rage she sensed in him now. Platitudes wouldn't work, but they were all she had to offer.

"Of course everything's different. Don't you think I know that?"

Baxter whined quietly in response to Gene's raised voice, but Lenae didn't hear a sound from Toby. Des had been carefully observing the pair, and he reinforced her belief that while Gene wasn't doing anything to alienate Toby, he also wasn't making any effort to bond with his dog. They performed well together, passing every test as they went through the course of training, but there was something missing. Lenae was frustrated by her inability to teach Gene the skills of partnership he needed. She could connect to her dogs, but not as easily with their owners. The ones who came with the excitement and drive necessary to have a successful experience with their dogs were easy enough for her—they did the main work of forming a working unit with their animals. Gene didn't want to need Toby.

"I understand," she said. And she did, but not in a way she could express to him. Cara had come into her life for what was supposed to be a brief moment, only to become more involved with the center's future than Lenae had anticipated. Lenae didn't *want* to want Cara in her life, didn't want to look forward to every puppy class and private consultation they would share together. She had accepted the offer of a little publicity, but events had gotten out of hand. Out of control.

She understood Gene's reluctance to follow where Toby was leading him, but she kept the connection to herself. After all, she hadn't lost her vision after a lifetime of seeing. She had been reluctant to appear dependent when she first got Baxter, but she hadn't been mourning a lost sense at the same time. She had no idea what to say to Gene that wouldn't sound condescending or as if she was downplaying his loss. *I've spent a lifetime not being able to see. If I can do it, you can, too.* "Give it some time, and I'm sure you and Toby will get to be good friends."

He didn't answer, and she didn't push the issue. The two of them were learning the city of Olympia and functioning well together, and she needed to be satisfied with the small victory. Maybe if she had matched him with one of the other dogs? She hated second-guessing herself already, with the first group of dogs and owners to come out of her training center. If she was making mistakes so soon, did she have any right to continue?

"This bistro has some great sandwiches and soups. There are also several different salads. We can ask the waitress for the specials when she comes to take our order."

"I've been here before," Gene repeated. "I've seen the menu."

Lenae rubbed her temple, suddenly wishing she'd suggested they meet in a bar instead of the bistro. She planned to eventually build several small cottages on her property so the new owners could live at the center while they learned to work with their dogs, and the money from Howard's grant would help that happen sooner than she had expected. But not soon enough to give Gene the constant encouragement and feedback he needed. For now, her clients stayed in a nearby hotel, first by themselves and eventually with their dogs. They met at the center for training classes, and out in the town for more informal, real-life practice.

Lenae ordered the pasta salad, and Gene asked for the same thing. He said he'd seen the menu before, but she wondered if he'd really *seen* it. How much of his anger was directed at himself, for not appreciating the gift of sight when he'd had it?

"Have you been having any trouble with Toby? Any difficulty getting him to follow your commands?" Might as well stick to the day-to-day realities of having a guide dog since he didn't seem ready yet to plumb any deeper.

"No. He does everything I ask." Gene paused. "He's a good dog."

Lenae tried to find solace in the softer tone Gene used in his last sentence. She had felt kindness in him from the first interview. She hadn't misjudged his character in that respect, at least.

"How are you doing with your pacing issues?" Lenae switched to this practical topic after their food was delivered. One that was quantifiable and unemotional. Gene and Toby always seemed to be a half-step off from each other. She had heard the disharmony when they walked on hard surfaces, and Des had confirmed her assessment of the pair.

"Better," Gene said. "I've been paying attention to the sound of his toenails on the pavement, like you said. I can count my steps now and match his stride better."

Gene sounded more comfortable with the new subject, but even such a mundane training problem nagged at Lenae. She'd never had one of her students need help matching stride with a dog. The transition in gait—once the visually impaired person adjusted to the dog's speed—seemed as natural as breathing to most people, partly because Lenae was careful to match dogs with owners based on normal stride length, but mostly because the two merged into one unit after the initial adjustment phase.

Gene and Toby were performing fine as separate individuals, but not as a team. Even Cara, in her short walk with Toby, had found a rhythm with him.

Cara again, entering her thoughts unbidden. Lenae heard the clink of Gene's fork hitting his plate several times, punctuated by his frustrated sighs, and she knew he was having trouble with his salad. Rather than give him suggestions she figured would be unwelcome, she kept on the topic of stride length. She described some new exercises for him to try even as she battled with doubt internally. She was a fine one for helping someone else correct his stride when she feared her preoccupation with Cara was throwing her off hers.

They got through lunch and some awkward conversation, and she was glad when her salad was finished and she was free to leave. She arranged for Gene to meet with Des that evening at his hotel—she wanted regular welfare checks on Toby, and she hoped Des would be able to reach Gene through all his anger. She certainly didn't seem able to do it. She was relieved to be back on the sidewalk, walking away from the bistro. Alone and safe—and in stride—with Baxter.

CHAPTER ELEVEN

Cara unleashed Pickwick in the yard behind the training center, and he catapulted himself into the wild group of puppies playing on the grass. The film crew for the network news was setting up hastily so they could get some footage of the melee. Cara would have preferred to attend this first puppy-walker class without the accompanying cameras and harsh lights since she had hundreds of questions for Lenae and wanted a chance to talk to the other walkers without being set apart as a media personality. She wanted to be just another volunteer, but instead of joining the others for cookies and talk about the puppies, she had to put up with combs and makeup brushes. Still, she had promised to do these weekly slots, and the benefits for the center would last far longer than her one-term puppy-walking stint.

Lenae was suffering through makeup and hair for the segment as well, and she appeared even less pleased with the process than Cara. Her light olive skin seemed unnaturally pale, and her posture was less formal than Cara had seen before. Baxter was pressed close against her left leg, as if he was supporting his tired owner. Cara waited until the news crew had left Lenae alone before she walked over.

"Hey. How are you?" Cara rested her hand lightly on Lenae's shoulder.

"About as exhausted as I must look, judging by your tone," Lenae said with a tight smile. She allowed Cara's touch for a few moments before she shifted away. "It's been a busy week, with introducing the owners to their dogs and doing orientation for this new set of puppy walkers. But it's part of the job. It'll only get more hectic as we start training more dogs each year."

Cara wondered how truthful Lenae's statements were. She figured the work must be time-consuming, but somehow Lenae seemed the type who would thrive on being busy. Her job as a writer for Three-N must have been a hundred times more demanding than this one. Something in her voice hinted at an emotional weariness, not a physical one. But Cara wouldn't pry.

"Sorry I seem to bring cameras everywhere I go, but the segment should be easy to film. Just do your normal orientation class, and after it's finished, I'll do a quick interview to talk about my week with Pickwick."

Normal. Lenae had no idea what a normal puppy walker class would be since she had never organized one before. All of her previous work had been one-on-one with individuals, helping them purchase and train a dog or learn to work with one they already had. She was a novice now, matching dogs with owners and guiding the puppies and their handlers through a vital and challenging year. Her confidence was already dented because of Gene and Toby's problems, so how could she assume she'd be any better at this part of the training?

"So, how was your week? Are you ready to quit yet?" Lenae was half joking, but she wouldn't have been surprised if Cara had shown up just to drop Pickwick back at the center. She had given Cara a puppy, believing Cara's priority was the good of the center and not her own advancement, and she hoped this wasn't yet another example of her inability to truly gauge character.

"No, I'm not ready to quit." Cara sounded hurt at the accusation, but there was a hint of something else behind it. "Although…"

Lenae had to laugh at the amount of exasperation Cara stuffed into that single word. "He's a handful, isn't he?"

"That's a drastic understatement. I'm buying energy drinks by the case, just so I can keep up with him."

"Trust me, I know. He was here at the center for two weeks before you got him, and he managed to get in plenty of mischief. He's an escape artist with extravagant tastes. He's eaten over five hundred dollars in shoes."

"He hasn't run up that high a tab with me yet, but I'm sure he'll find some way to break into my closet. If I'd listened to Des and been more careful with my good sneakers, I'd still be able to go jogging every day."

"How do you think Des learned the lesson? Those were his shoes that Pickwick ate."

Cara joined in her laughter, and Lenae inexplicably found some of her tension ease. She still had doubts, but somehow the liquid sound of Cara's laugh—joined with her own throatier chuckle—made everything seem better for a brief moment. Commiseration, a relief from loneliness. All illusions, Lenae was sure, but still, she'd accept the temporary lightening of her mood.

Once the cameras were on, however, Cara's voice and laugh transformed subtly. Certainly no less sweet, but not as carefree. Lenae thought she heard a tightening in Cara's throat, and her own tensed in response. Cara joked and chatted with the other puppy walkers—two teenagers working on a 4-H project, a middle-aged couple sharing the responsibility, and two graduate-school friends of Des—as they all asked a ton of questions and shared stories about their little hell-raisers, but Cara had definitely changed. The others sounded more nervous and stilted in front of the cameras than they had been before, but their inflections and personalities stayed the same. Not Cara.

A few minutes ago, Lenae had been certain that, no matter how much she had denied it, Cara wanted this opportunity to shine, to move beyond her small-time public TV show and possibly vie for a position as a reporter, then an anchor. But now, hearing Cara shift from one moment to the next, Lenae wasn't so sure.

It wasn't that Cara sounded uncomfortable or unhappy as she finished up her interview. No, she spoke easily and answered questions without hesitating or groping for words. She was bright and cheerful. But while she was praising the couple for their well-behaved puppy and questioning them about their previous puppy-walking experiences, Lenae recognized that Cara somehow… dimmed herself. Closed off something of the exuberant, singing-at-the-top-of-her-lungs Cara, so the focus fell on the people she was interviewing.

Lenae thought back to her own interview for Cara's show. Except for the brief moment when she and Cara had disagreed about the puppy walkers, Cara had made sure the dogs and Lenae or Des were always center stage. For as much as she was charismatic and chatty with the camera, she made sure the show was about them, not about herself. That wasn't the behavior of someone trying to climb the media ladder. That wasn't the behavior of someone just using Lenae or the center. Was it? Wasn't Cara showing her real self—the person who cared deeply about the causes she promoted?

Lenae wasn't sure what to believe about Cara anymore. She thought she had pinned down her character from the start. A self-absorbed, ambitious rising star. After spending time with her, she had revised her initial assumptions. She had discovered Cara's humor in her ability to laugh at herself. She'd seen Cara's commitment and her obvious love of animals. But even when she had been in Cara's house, she hadn't learned about the core of her.

Cara had described the rooms where she prepared for her teaching job and where she researched subjects for her show. But those pursuits were for other people. Cara hadn't talked about hobbies or mementos as she gave Lenae the tour of her house. And while Cara had had a personal and intense response to the idea of puppy walking during their first interview, Lenae hadn't seen that fire in her again. Lenae felt an unaccustomed desire to see more emotion from her. To provoke it somehow. Cara was excellent at bringing out the passion and interesting qualities in others, but Lenae wondered what stirred Cara's own passion.

The puppy-walking class came to a halt and the cameras stopped rolling. Lenae staunched her twinge of disappointment. Whatever passion was hiding beneath Cara's calm and serene professional surface would have to remain hidden, at least for now.

CHAPTER TWELVE

Cara slowed down for the turn, checking in her rearview mirror to make sure her entire caravan was still with her, and pulled into the driveway to Lenae's training center. Pickwick sat beside her, covering the passenger-side window with nose prints as he strained to get a view of the outside world. She was convinced he recognized that he was back at the center since he usually spent drives attempting to devour her floor mats or seat cushions, although Lenae had spent most of their first two puppy-walking classes giving advice on how to keep the pups from chewing inappropriately. Cara hoped the rest of the volunteers had benefitted from the suggestions, but Pickwick seemed determined to resist them all.

She slowly drove toward the office with two cars and a minivan behind her. She'd never gotten a formal answer to her student's question—how a person could help the center without a significant time commitment—because once she'd thought about it, the answer was glaringly obvious. In the broken, chipped-paint-covered fence around the training area, in the weedy and neglected gardens, and in the patchy lawn. She had mentioned the disrepair to her class, and the twelve students had immediately started planning a weekend work party. Now they, plus a few more recruits, were armed with paint and rakes and a thatcher and were ready to descend on the center.

Cara had wanted to surprise Lenae with the help, but she had told Des about her plan. He had arranged a time when the grounds would be quiet and empty enough for them to work. Cara parked in front of the house and waved for the rest of the group to wait while she went to find Lenae.

She tapped on the partially open office door and went inside. Baxter met her as she walked down the hall, and Cara let Pickwick off his leash to play with the older dog. Lenae was at her desk, without musical accompaniment this time, and her fingers moved rapidly over a piece of paper. Cara marveled again at the dexterity and sensitivity of Lenae's fingertips, able to discern and translate simple dots into complex words and sentences. Fingertips that would be able to sense nuances of feeling and response.

"Good morning, Lenae," she said, clearing her throat as the thought of Lenae touching her made it difficult to speak.

"Cara, hello. What brings you here? Is everything all right with Pickwick?" The puppy bounded over to greet her, and Lenae bent down to pet him.

"He's doing well. Full of energy as you can probably tell." Pickwick left Lenae's side, went over to Baxter, and started chewing on his ears. "I came today because my students met Pickwick and wanted to help the center in some way. I told them about some of the repairs you needed done around here, and we've come ready to paint and weed and mend fences."

"Without letting me know."

Cara was getting accustomed to Lenae's shifts from warm and seemingly happy to see her and Pickwick to icy cold, but Cara had only heard crystals in Lenae's tone, now and again, never before such a blizzard.

"This is a working center, and I have students and dogs in training full-time now."

"I talked to Des to make sure we wouldn't be intruding during a class," Cara said, her voice stiffening in response to Lenae's censure. "He thought it was a great idea and said the assistance would be appreciated."

Lenae tapped her fingernail on her desk, finding a soft spot in the grainy wood and digging her nail into it. She had meant to defend her lack of ambition in the cosmetic details of her center by telling Cara how busy she'd been lately—not to imply that Cara and her work crew would be interrupting a class. But busyness didn't explain why the fences were broken and the gardens were bare patches.

Lenae could do most things on her own—and she had fought for independence and self-sufficiency since she had taken her first steps as a toddler—but there were frustrating aspects of this career that forced her to rely on other people. Des had to be a set of eyes for her, a necessary observer and assistant who was able to watch the owners and dogs work together. And the television crews and volunteers and donors required to make the center a success apparently couldn't see past the appearance of the place to the actual work she was doing here. She needed help. And, damn it, the more she needed it, the more she hated the offer. Especially from Cara. She wanted Cara of all people to think of her as an equal, not as a charity case. To see her as a passionate and capable woman, not as a weak and disabled one. She sounded ungrateful, but she couldn't stop her defensive reaction. Cara had looked around her center and had seen Lenae's weaknesses.

She turned to face Cara. "I told Des we'd get to those minor repairs after we got the training sessions going. It's not a priority right now. He might think it is, but the dogs and their owners matter more than having pretty flowers in the garden."

"I get what you're saying. You do something meaningful here. So let me and my students take care of some of the petty details and free up your time for training."

"I didn't mean…I understand that to sighted people these things matter…"

Cara frowned. Lenae might as well come right out and say *I'm doing vital and important work here. You're doing nothing more than glossing over the surface of life, like you always do.* Okay, maybe some of Cara's own feelings were influencing her response, but she didn't need Lenae pointing out that she was deep while Cara was shallow.

"Right. Because you're so deep, but we're all mindless and superficial. Do you want the help, or not? I can tell everyone to go and leave you alone."

Cara was backing toward the door when Lenae stood and reached out a hand. She was tempted to stay out of range or just walk away, but she couldn't resist Lenae's offer or her own need to make contact. She took two steps forward and touched Lenae's fingers with her own. The contact was brief, and both moved away at the same time, but the connection seemed to soften the atmosphere even as it sent heat up Cara's arm and into her chest.

"I'd like your help," Lenae said, as if each word hurt to say.

"But you don't want to admit it?" Cara understood. She'd learned not to accept favors from her family or from others she met in the media business. The strings attached to them were as binding as shackles. "I get that, Lenae. No strings, I promise."

Lenae didn't answer the question. "Tell your students I said thank you."

Cara wanted to touch Lenae again, but she kept her distance. "Why don't you tell them yourself? They'd love to meet you."

"I have work to do." Lenae sat at her desk again. "But I'll come out later and check on your progress."

"We'll try not to disappoint you," Cara said, smiling as she spoke so her tone would be playful and teasing.

Lenae hesitated, and then seemed to accept the change in mood. "I hope not. I can be a strict taskmaster."

"I'm sure you can," Cara said, her mind going directly to the bedroom. She'd let Lenae be the boss as long as she made good use of those dexterous fingers. The shy smile that replaced Lenae's frown made her wonder if Lenae's thoughts had gone in the same direction. "Luckily, I do my best work under pressure. Come on, Pickwick, let's go."

❖

As soon as Cara left, Lenae picked up the paper she had been reading, but her hands were still. She'd felt more comfortable with the joking mood than with Cara's earnest attempts to help her. Weak. She didn't want to be seen as weak or helpless in anyone's eyes, but especially not Cara's. But she could be strong in the moments when Cara flirted because she knew they weren't real. They were part of the Cara who showed up for the cameras. The one who carefully controlled what other people saw and heard. Lenae wouldn't take the sexy teasing seriously, but still… it was a pleasant distraction.

Lenae stayed inside her office for almost an hour, but she didn't get anything done except replay her conversation with Cara, carrying the banter further in her mind—all the way to bed. She had reached out her hand to Cara in apology, not expecting her response to the quick, casual touch. Instead of simply feeling Cara at the point of contact, Lenae's entire body had responded to her. Warm, yearning. She heard the shouts and laughter through the open window as Cara and her students worked in the yard. The rhythmic beat of hammers proved that they were as industrious as they were playful. Lenae heard the click of Baxter's nails as he walked back and forth between his bed and the window, and she finally gave in to his obvious desire to be outside in the sunshine and part of the activity. Because he had been cooped up all morning, not because she had been straining to distinguish Cara's voice and laugh from all the others.

She and Baxter stepped onto the porch and Pickwick—oblivious to Baxter's harness and his role as a working guide dog—met them with a flurry of puppy yips and jumped on her leg.

"Down, Pickwick," she said in a calm voice. "Can you sit?" She pushed forward with her leg and snapped her fingers above his head. She knew the combined motions would put him slightly off balance toward his rear. He'd be staring at her fingers as they snapped and would naturally sit down as he looked up. She reached down to scratch his ears and found, no surprise, that he was actually sitting. "What a good boy!"

"How the hell did you do that?" Cara glared at the traitorous puppy. She had been watching for Lenae to emerge from her office for at least an hour, finding any excuse to work close to the old house, while Pickwick attempted to demolish everything Cara repaired. "I've been working for *days* on getting him not to jump on me, and I figured it'd be a few more weeks before I could get him to do something as obedient as sitting. You didn't even tell him what to do, you just suggested it."

"The key to training is putting the dog in a place where the right behavior comes naturally. If you're constantly fighting him, it'll always be a struggle, but if you can get the response you want while making him think it was his idea in the first place, then it's much easier on both of you. Don't worry, we'll go over these techniques in our classes."

Cara laughed at the notion of outsmarting a puppy as she patted Pickwick on the head. He turned to look back at her and rolled out of his seated position and onto his side. "Amazing. I'm sure you'll be able to teach me some training aids, but you have a knack for communicating with these dogs. Skills can be taught, but talent is inborn."

"Like yours."

Cara straightened up. Was Lenae kidding? She hadn't done anything around Lenae except report on her training center in front of the camera. Even bringing the students here today hadn't been her doing—she'd merely talked about the positive work Lenae was doing, and they had wanted to help. "I don't have any special abilities like you do. I spend my life sharing stories about people who use their time and talent to help others, but I don't do anything of my own."

One of the students stopped near them to ask Cara a question about paint colors, and Lenae sat on a bench while half-listening to the conversation and playing with Pickwick. She moved her hand to find him when he scooted away, and she bumped into a wooden box sitting next to her. She felt along the sides and top. A hanging basket. Cara must have been putting it up near the office door when Lenae had come out. She touched the plants and felt one with velvety leaves, one with delicately soft petals, and one with tiny, tight leaves and buds. She rubbed her palm over a needlelike, upright plant.

"That's rosemary," Cara said. "Smell your hand."

Lenae sniffed her palm. She had used rosemary for cooking plenty of times but somehow had never really associated the culinary herb with a live and growing plant. Too much time in the city. "I've never gotten into gardening before. I think weeding would be a challenge."

Lenae almost gasped out loud when Cara took her hand. She felt the tickle of Cara's breath and the fleeting touch of her nose and mouth as Cara shared the lingering scent. Cara moved Lenae's unresisting hand to another plant in the hanging basket. "This one is sage. Pull off a leaf and crush it in your hand before you smell it. And I'll bet you could come up with some ways to tell the difference between weeds and plants if you wanted to garden. You could plant flowers or herbs in evenly spaced rows and just weed around them, or memorize how your plants smell and feel. It's a great hobby, whether you just want to get in touch with the earth, or you want to use what you grow for cooking."

Lenae struggled to discern anything besides the sensation of Cara's touch. She plucked a fuzzy leaf and rubbed it between her fingers, with Cara's hand still cradling hers. Lenae raised both of their hands to her face and inhaled deeply. The earthy scent of sage mingled with her own sophisticated Chanel and Cara's citrus notes to create a cacophony of aromas. Lenae felt Cara's fingers lightly graze her cheek before she dropped their contact. Lenae missed her touch with an odd ache, but their combined scents still lingered in her mind.

"What are the others?" Lenae asked quietly, not wanting to break the illusion of being alone with Cara in an enchanted garden. The noise of hammering and shouting faded into the background.

"This is thyme, and the flowers are geraniums." Cara guided Lenae's hand to the different plants. "I tried to pick plants that had different textures and scents so you'd enjoy them, and they're all edible as well. Just pick off a few leaves if you want to use them for cooking."

"How thoughtful. I love it," Lenae said. She tried to cover her surprise at the effort Cara had put into the small basket by leaning over to sniff the thyme. She had assumed the cosmetic improvements wouldn't affect her at all, but Cara had taken the time to ensure that Lenae could share in the activities of the day. She concentrated on the lemony, woodsy herb. Yes, a thoughtful gesture. Nothing more. Cara couldn't have any idea how erotic the combination of aroma and touch was to her.

"Maybe Baxter and I should go get lunch for everyone," Lenae said. She needed to get off this porch, do something practical. Anything to keep from thinking about the way Cara had touched her hand when Cara had leaned close to smell the sage. Or the way Lenae's skin had felt energized with electricity when Cara touched her cheek. She felt a little guilty for having been so defensive when Cara and the students arrived, and way too pleased by Cara's gesture with the tactile and fragrant basket. Some time by herself, with Baxter, would help her get the messier emotions under control.

"Great idea," Cara said. "Pickwick and I will come with you."

CHAPTER THIRTEEN

Cara lengthened her stride to keep up with Lenae and Baxter's quick pace. Pickwick did his usual dart back-and-forth across the sidewalk, threatening to tangle her in his leash, while Baxter marched along with purpose, carefully leading Lenae around people and obstacles. She was glad to have the distractions, though, to keep her mind occupied. She had come up with the idea of Lenae's hanging basket because she thought Lenae might appreciate the different qualities of the herbs, but she hadn't anticipated the scene she'd just experienced. The smell of sex, the feel of skin—those were as much a part of sensual encounters for Cara as was sight. But merely sharing the plants with Lenae had aroused her beyond anything she had felt before. Every sense had come alive with the subtle onslaught of fragrance and texture.

"I can't imagine Pickwick will ever be able to do this job like Baxter does," she said, trying to control her voice and hide how out of breath she was after three short blocks. "He has no attention span. He'll run his person right into a lamppost."

Lenae laughed. "He has the attention span of a puppy. We won't put him into training until he's mature enough to handle it, but you'll be surprised by the differences you'll see in him after a year. And remember that the more difficult puppies often make the best guide dogs since they're intelligent and willing to take initiative. I've kept in touch with Baxter's puppy walker, Lynn, and she's told me some hilarious stories about what a handful he was when he was a pup."

"I guess I'll have to trust you on this since it's your area of expertise, but I'm still skeptical." Cara unwound the leash after Pickwick wove between the legs of a mailbox. At least Pickwick seemed calmer around Baxter than he did when they were alone. She had offered to come with Lenae to get lunch for the students because she wanted to spend more time with Lenae, to maintain the connection she'd felt when holding Lenae's herb-scented hand. Her feelings about Lenae were too complicated to be comfortable, though. Lenae's career choice and her dedication to her center were admirable, but they made Cara feel self-centered by comparison. Even though she wasn't as hungry for fame and attention as her family, she was still a professional pretty face. Sure, she was selling her audience on the causes she featured on her show, encouraging them to support good works, instead of selling herself out for commercial television, but the jobs were basically the same. Empty smiles for the camera. Philanthropy that ended when the producer said *Cut*.

"Maybe," Lenae said after remaining silent for a long moment.

"Maybe…what?" Cara asked, confused since she had been startled out of her own thoughts. "Maybe Pickwick will be a good guide dog?"

"No. I meant maybe training is my area of expertise. I'm still not sure."

"Really?" Cara hadn't expected Lenae to have doubts about what she was doing. She was even more surprised that Lenae would admit to them. "But look at what a partnership you've built with Baxter, and how well you trained Toby. I was helpless with the blindfold on, but he took care of me every step of the way. Because of the training you gave him."

Baxter stopped in front of the deli, and Lenae felt for the handle and opened the door. Cara let the conversation end while she and Lenae stood near the counter and decided what kind of sub sandwiches to order. The smells of vinegar and cured meat must have been tempting to dog noses, and Cara knew Lenae heard Pickwick's front claws scratching on the glass-fronted case of meats and cheeses. Cara struggled with him and cursed under her breath.

"Maybe I should take him outside," Cara said when they had placed their order.

"He needs to get accustomed to being in restaurants and other tempting places," Lenae said.

Cara knew this was true. Pickwick *did* need to learn self-control. But she wondered if Lenae was deliberately turning the conversation away from her own insecurities to her comfort zone of puppy training.

"He'll eventually learn to keep focused on you and not on the food he can smell, but only after plenty of exposure. Why don't you find us a table near the door, and we'll see if he'll settle down when Baxter does."

Lenae let go of Baxter's harness once she sat down, and he immediately lay down under her chair. Cara watched Pickwick bump against Lenae's ankles as he tried to goad the older dog into a wrestling match. When Baxter's only response was a deep sigh, Pickwick gave up and sat down on Lenae's foot.

"He's chewing on Baxter's harness," Cara said. She knew she should do more to stop him than just telling Lenae and making it her problem, but she hadn't been able to get through to the puppy yet. Let the expert handle him since she was sitting right there. Besides, she loved seeing Lenae's assuredness when she worked with the dogs. Cara admired the combination of passion and skill that Lenae—and most of her other *Around the Sound* interviewees—possessed.

"Do you have a chew toy for him?"

Cara always had one with her, although Pickwick didn't seem to care. She put the bone-shaped toy in Lenae's waiting hand.

"First, make it uncomfortable for him to keep chewing on the inappropriate object," Lenae said, switching from her conversational tone into what Cara was starting to recognize as her teaching voice. Patient and reassuring. Seemingly unaffected by the way they'd touched earlier. She watched as Lenae felt for Pickwick's busy mouth. "Be prepared for those sharp little teeth, and put light pressure on his tongue. Just enough to be annoying to him."

Pickwick let go of the harness as he poked his tongue out and seemed like he was trying to spit Lenae's hand out of his mouth. She immediately praised him when he dropped the harness, and offered him the chew toy. He refused it, but after repeating the same process several times, he finally took the toy from her and curled up next to Baxter's head while he chomped on it.

"Well, now you're just showing off," Cara said. She wasn't sure what was most impressive—the sight of Pickwick doing a reasonable impression of a well-behaved puppy, or Lenae's intuitive way of making him want to be one. "If you can teach people as easily as you do dogs, I'll bet you'll have me obeying your every whim before we get our sandwiches."

"People aren't as straightforward as animals, but I can give it a try. Maybe I can get you to quack like a duck whenever I say the word *action*. That'd be amusing the next time you film a puppy-walking spot."

Cara sensed something behind Lenae's laughter. A subtle denigration of Cara's profession? Or was the uneasiness associated with Lenae and not her? She went against her own instincts and assumed Lenae was thinking of her own career, not Cara's. "Joking aside, you truly have a gift. Training in any capacity, whether human or animal, is admirable when it's done with kindness and finesse."

"Thank you." Lenae relaxed her facial muscles. She had read and heard about people's emotions being conveyed through expression, but the concept was foreign to her. She could feel a frown or a smile through her fingertips, but she had no idea how her own face registered her feelings to a sighted person. So over the years she had figured out how to put on a mask of stillness. The ability had served well in the cutthroat world of news writing, and she had often been praised for having a good poker face. But now, in her new capacity as teacher—especially someone striving to help her students develop the bonds of trust and partnership with other beings—the skill of hiding her thoughts might be a liability.

Calm facial muscles, but an internal struggle. Lenae hadn't even voiced her doubts to Des, but she sensed Cara might somehow understand her feelings of inadequacy.

"I appreciate the compliment. I'm fine with the dogs," she said, not wanting to sound boastful, but being honest about the results she'd had in the past. "Working with Baxter, and later with the few guide dogs I trained, I felt…I don't know. Right. Like the answers to behavioral problems or next steps in training just came into my head when I needed them. I really believe the methods I've developed will be successful when I have the chance to implement them from early stages forward."

"But…?"

"But I don't work nearly as well with people. I guess I did well when the cases were easy. The students I had in the past were all highly motivated to connect with a guide dog. They had committed money and time and sought me out because they didn't have access to more conventional training centers."

"How is it different now? Aren't the new owners here because they want a dog?"

Lenae wrestled with her explanation. "Usually. But sometimes they'll come here because a doctor or therapist has recommended it. Or they need the independence to get a job or to live alone. But it's not as simple as grabbing hold of the harness and saying the correct commands." Lenae struggled to find a way to explain the experience without telling her personal story. She couldn't get past the worry that Cara might exploit it someday—not because of a meanness of spirit, but if she saw an opportunity to use the information as a way to promote the show, and her career. Lenae had been through that before, and she was determined to protect herself from being a stepping stone ever again.

"Think about your afternoon walk with Toby. How many different emotions did you feel during that short time?"

Lenae thought back to the day they had filmed the segment. She hadn't realized then, as she'd argued with Cara over the motives and compassion of the puppy walkers, that she'd be here now with Cara, with Pickwick flopped against their feet. If she hadn't been sure of Cara's ability to remain detached, sure of Cara's respect for the process, she'd never have agreed to let Pickwick train with her. During that walk with Toby, Cara had shown compassion and understanding.

"Fear," Cara said, breaking into Lenae's thoughts. "We were moving so fast, and I had no idea whether I was about to trip over something or get run over. But more than physical danger, I was afraid of moving through darkness with only the wood of the harness connecting me to the world. I'm sorry. Maybe I shouldn't have said that. I know you live with this every—"

"You're right, Cara. I do live with it, but I remember getting Baxter and how different movement was from what I was accustomed to. I hadn't realized how slowly and carefully I walked through life until I took hold of his harness, and off we went. It was terrifying—like you said, not just in a physical way, but in a sense of how much my life would change with this wonderful creature by my side. But what else did you feel?"

"I remember when Toby moved me back onto the sidewalk when I almost tripped off the curb. The connection with him was awesome. I also felt pride because I was learning something new, and a sense of sympathy as I got a chance to experience a small part of someone else's world. I'll admit I was relieved when I was able to take the blindfold off and return to my normal, but I also was kind of sad since I knew I'd never have the strong connection to a partner like you have with Baxter, and like I had a taste of with Toby."

Lenae was impressed by Cara's honesty and by her ability to discern the complex feelings she had experienced. She had thought, after hearing Cara talk on camera, that she would be less...dimensional. More focused on what was visible on film and less on her internal life. "Now imagine all those emotions, but magnified. You're changing your whole way of life. And maybe you've recently lost your sight and you haven't yet come to terms with it."

"It would be overwhelming. I'm not sure how I'd react, but some of those emotions would have to break free, even if I tried very hard to control them."

Lenae agreed. She and Cara both seemed able to control their inner lives and carefully choose what would be revealed to the outer world. "I can deal with the responses and reactions of the dogs because they usually make sense if you try to understand them. But I have a harder time with the people. I honestly don't know if I'll be able to get past my inability to read and communicate with humans. I was a writer, and I didn't have trouble expressing difficult concepts and news stories and political issues through words, but this is different. I'm not trying to explain the way to train a guide dog, but I'm trying to explain how to *feel* trust and love. How to create a partnership. And I'm failing."

"You're helping me with Pickwick. And I'll bet most of your students are doing just fine. Who's the one who recently lost vision?"

Lenae should have known Cara would pick up on the heart of her problem. She might not be working for a big network, but she was a reporter at heart.

"His name is Gene, and I matched him with Toby. I was so certain they'd be a good match—well, to be honest, I was convinced I had some sort of sixth sense when it came to pairing dogs and owners. I was proud of it. But I messed up with these two. He's still raging over the loss of his sight, but he won't admit it. And you and Toby formed a better partnership in one hour than they have in over a week. They do their jobs together, but there's no sense of the…whatever it is between me and Baxter and between my other students and their dogs. I can't define or describe it well, so I can't teach it to him."

Cara had felt a hint of the bond Lenae was talking about, but she had even less experience with it than Lenae. She'd never felt it in a real or lasting way with a person or animal, but she had no doubt she'd know it if it happened to her. She just didn't believe it ever would. She'd had a brief glimpse of an all-encompassing connection today with Lenae—when every sense was attuned to the other person—but it had been temporary and probably one-sided. "Maybe it's like falling in love. You've arranged the pairings, but the emotional attachment might take its own time to develop. I don't think you can force it."

Cara heard Lenae's sigh. Frustration and doubt. She figured Lenae had felt plenty of the first in her life, but Lenae didn't seem like the type to have much self-doubt.

"I'm trying to have patience," Lenae said. "To keep telling myself and Gene not to worry, that it will eventually be okay. But I don't know if either of us believes me."

Cara imagined the blindfold she had been wearing when she walked with Toby. What if she had been told she could never take it off? Would she be content to listen to promises that she'd eventually learn to cope? "Maybe it won't be okay," she said before she could stop herself.

"What do you mean? He'll have to adjust to his condition and move on. It's part of life. Things don't always work out like we want, but we adapt and keep going."

"You're right that he will have to face the fact that he can't change things, but focusing on the positive might not help him right now. Maybe he needs to be allowed to feel exactly what he feels, as long as Toby is safe with him and they're functioning well enough. Don't deny who he is at this moment, or what he's experiencing."

Lenae wasn't convinced. The sooner Gene accepted his lot in life, the sooner he'd be able to move on and get back to the world of the living. He was isolated in his pain, not allowing Toby or anyone else to get close. It wasn't a healthy way to live, Lenae knew from experience. She kept people away as much as she could, but at least she had allowed Baxter close to her. She carried the bags of sandwiches back to the center while Cara struggled to control Pickwick, who was refreshed after his short nap at the deli. She didn't believe Cara's advice would work in her situation, but she was curious at the emotion she'd detected behind it. Had Cara ever been allowed to truly be herself, or had her authentic thoughts and feelings been criticized, made to be kept under wraps? Lenae most likely wouldn't have a chance to find out. Today was a moment out of time, and after Cara's students left, her time with Cara would be limited to puppy-walking sessions—always documented by camera and lacking any of the depth hinted at in today's conversation or by the sensuality of sharing the hanging basket. Their relationship would return to normal, as flat as a television screen.

CHAPTER FOURTEEN

Lenae pulled on a pair of jeans and a hooded sweatshirt. The Washington morning was misty and colder than usual for autumn, but she loved the feel of moisture on her skin. The mild, damp climate of the Northwest suited her more than her childhood home in Southern California or her more recent home in New York City, where she'd worked for Three-N. Baxter didn't mind the wet, either, and they'd often go for long walks alone in the rain. Even with his raincoat, he'd stop every once in a while and shake drops of water all over her, soaking her more than the weather did. Today, though, they wouldn't be sharing a walk in peace and solitude. They'd have six hyperactive puppies along with them.

Lenae had been alternating between looking forward to the outing and feeling misgivings about it all morning. She had shared too much with Cara to feel comfortable in her presence. First, Cara had noticed Lenae needed help with the yard and fencing. Second, Lenae had admitted she was having issues with one of her clients. Opening up like that to any person was a sign of weakness and dependence—vulnerabilities that left her in danger of being manipulated or, worse, pitied. But to talk so honestly with a reporter? Insanity. At the very least, Cara might not respect her as a trainer anymore. At worst, Lenae's problems might become tonight's news.

She buckled a clear plastic raincoat over Baxter's service-dog cape and stuffed a few puppy-sized coats in her pocket in case any of the walkers forgot them. She combed her hair as a small concession to the cameras that would be following their every move. The gesture would be made meaningless by the rain, but Lenae didn't want to hear Des make any comments about her appearance.

At least he was pleased by the results of Cara's efforts to help with the yard. Lenae could feel the difference in the lawn, and Des was ecstatic about the fence and garden. One of Cara's students, Nancy, had even returned a few times to maintain the flowers she'd planted around the office. Lenae had to admit she enjoyed the scent of them every time she walked out the front door. Cara's herbs were her favorites, though, and she often added a small pinch of sage or rosemary even to her microwaved meals for a touch of elegance and a reminder of Cara.

As if she needed reminders of Cara. She was everywhere in Lenae's mind, tangled up in scents and sensations. Lenae had let her defenses down after their physical connection, and she had talked too freely about her problems with Gene. Lenae had been burned before when she had revealed professional information in her private life. She didn't believe Cara would try to harm her by revealing business issues on air, but Cara might not realize how damaging the information about Gene—and Lenae's self-doubts—could be. Cara had come in as a volunteer under unusual circumstances, and they had bonded in their desire not to be unwitting victims of Howard Bradley's plans. They were doing what he had wanted, each for her own reasons.

But she could never forget that Cara was a volunteer for the center, not her new confidante. She needed to take control of herself and her training classes. No more admitting she was failing with Gene or having trouble managing the upkeep of her own property. Even though her self-confidence was sagging because one of her matches was seemingly unsuccessful—a full one-third of her first training class—she had to keep her doubts about her abilities from affecting the way she handled the other phases of training. She had made a plan for the puppy-walking classes to follow, and she couldn't start second-guessing herself after just one week.

"Hi, Lenae," Des greeted her as soon as she entered the office. She let Baxter loose for his morning wrestle, and she felt her way over to the desk. A wet nose gently pressed against her hand, and she knelt to visit with the quiet dog.

"Good morning, Gem. Are you ready for training today?" The soft-coated Lab wagged her whole body in excitement, making her raincoat crinkle with her movement, but Des sounded less sure.

"She hates to get wet," he said. "She'll be dragging me from awning to awning all day."

Lenae laughed as Gem licked her face. "Maybe the puppies will annoy her enough when she takes cover that she'll prefer getting rained on to hiding away from the weather with them."

Lenae knew the moment when Cara came into the room, even before she heard Pickwick join the Des-and-Baxter wrestling match. She wasn't sure what triggered her awareness—a subconscious hint of her creamy perfume or the unique fall of her footsteps? She was always attuned to her environment, but her awareness seemed unnaturally high where Cara was concerned.

"Hey, are you saying my sweet puppy is *annoying*? I can't believe it, can you, Pickwick?"

Cara knelt, close enough so Lenae felt their thighs touch. And she had thought having contact with Cara's hand was enticing.

"Good morning, Lenae. Who's this beautiful girl?" Cara petted the Lab, her fingers tangling with Lenae's. "Did I meet her when we filmed the show?"

"Only briefly." Lenae stood and straightened her hair and clothes, putting everything back in place. If only she could tame her scattered emotions as easily. "That's Gem. She's right out of her puppy-walking phase, but she belongs to Des now. We'll try for some puppies from her when she's a little older."

"You're kidding, right?" Cara asked. Lenae heard disbelief in her tone. "Pickwick will be this well-behaved when I have to give him back?"

"Well," Des answered from the floor. Lenae heard Pickwick's distinctive tiny growl and figured Des was being mauled by the puppy in question. "We don't have such high expectations for him."

"Or me, by implication," Cara said with a laugh. "I'd be offended, but I tend to agree with you. Can you hold him still while I try to get this blasted raincoat on him? He hates the sound it makes."

"Come here, Pickwick," Lenae said, kneeling on the floor again. She held out her hand for the raincoat as the puppy obediently trotted to her. "He needs to get accustomed to the plastic, not only for the times it rains, but because he'll be around bags and umbrellas and raincoats all year round."

Pickwick sat patiently next to Lenae and let her wad up the plastic and rub it all over him before she buckled it in place. She heard a muttered comment from Cara that sounded like *blasted puppy* before he stood up, shook himself with a clatter of raincoat and scratch of toenails on the floor, and trotted over to greet Gem.

"It really bugs me when you do that," Cara said. Lenae recognized hints of frustration in her half-joking, half-in-earnest voice.

"Don't be too tentative with him or he won't respect you," Lenae said, thinking she needed to take her own advice and be assertive in today's class. Not let Cara or the others see her as weak. She stood again and called Baxter to her. "Have the others arrived yet? Or your camera crew?"

"No cameras today," Cara said, with what sounded like a relieved sigh. "Pickwick and I filmed our segment in Seattle yesterday, so I'd be able to focus on class today and not on performing."

Lenae wasn't sure what to say in response. From the start, she had hoped Cara would fulfill her puppy-walking duties in spite of the cameras around her, but she hadn't expected Cara to go out of her way like this. Cara was more serious about her duties than Lenae had ever expected, and she was impressed—and she thought she owed Cara an apology for ever underestimating her commitment. She was trying to find a way to say those things to Cara when she heard the rest of the puppy walkers coming through the front door.

"Thank you," she said, hoping Cara might understand how much she meant by the simple words. Cara gave her arm a light squeeze of acknowledgment as Lenae walked past her. Lenae exhaled at her casual touch, caught by surprise yet again at her body's immediate response.

❖

"You're welcome," Cara said, even though Lenae had already left the office. Lenae had seemed surprised she'd come without cameras—surprised, but deeply pleased.

Cara joined the rest of the puppy walkers, happy to be solo today and not surrounded by booms and cameras. She took a seat near the front of the room—instead of hiding in the back to be unobtrusive as usual—and let Pickwick romp with the other puppies. She noticed all of them had their raincoats on and wondered if no one else had needed assistance getting the simple garment on their dog. Part of her liked watching Lenae work with Pickwick, however. Lenae's skills were undeniable, and Cara admired her easy way with the dogs. After a week alone with Pickwick, she appreciated Lenae's help. More than that, she felt a curious sense of pride when she saw Lenae's training talent in action. Cara had felt admiration for the people she interviewed, and sometimes an emotion bordering on envy, but it was different with Lenae. More personal, as if Lenae's successes belonged in some small part to her, too. Cara was happy to joke about her own misguided attempts to manage Pickwick because her clumsiness underscored Lenae's abilities.

Each member of the group reported on their previous week, and Cara was relieved that she wasn't the only one facing challenges. If this had been a room full of well-behaved dogs and competent handlers, she'd have been ready to give up and quit, but everyone had questions and funny stories about their puppies.

"As I'm sure you've noticed, I don't have cameras watching my every move this week," Cara said when it was her turn to talk. "I wanted to have today free to concentrate on Pickwick, so I decided to take him to Seattle yesterday. We met the camera crew down by Pike Place, and they filmed me pretending to buy vegetables and fish while Pickwick walked with me. After they edit out the footage of him tripping people with his leash and stealing money out of a street musician's guitar case, I doubt they'll have much to use."

Lenae laughed along with the rest of the group. "What else did you do while you were in the city?" she asked.

"Well…" Cara drew the word out for several syllables. She loved watching Lenae's face relax into laughter, when her stress lines eased and her lips looked soft and pliant, so Cara launched into another humorous Pickwick anecdote. "I thought it would be fun to take him to the aquarium. I haven't been in years, and it seemed like a quiet way to spend the afternoon. Pickwick, however, had no intention of being quiet. He barked at every fish and sea animal he saw, he dragged me past the underground tanks like he was being chased by sharks, and he got loose near the hands-on exhibit and ran off with a sea anemone in his mouth."

"He did not!" Lenae exclaimed, her voice sounding torn between horror and amusement at Pickwick's antics.

"Okay, I made up the part about the anemone," Cara admitted. "But the rest is true. He barked until he could barely croak out another sound, and believe me, it echoes in that place. I'm surprised no one asked us to leave."

Lenae wiped tears of laughter from her eyes. "How about we skip the aquariums today, but we'll plan on getting all the puppies to one in the future. Sounds like a great training opportunity."

"Or lack-of-training opportunity," Des added.

"Very funny. Pickwick and I are offended," Cara said. She wanted to spin stories all day long if they made Lenae laugh so hard.

"Pickwick seems none the worse for the experience." Nor, Lenae noted, was Cara. She loved how totally unfazed Cara sounded by the jokes and laughter. She was doing her best with Pickwick, but she didn't mind sharing her mistakes. Lenae admired that quality in Cara, even if she couldn't afford to have it herself.

"Hopefully today will be a tamer excursion," she said. "Des will drive us to downtown Olympia in the center's van, so we can practice riding on public transportation. He'll also be bringing Gem along and will explain the training she's going through right now. She's recently out of her puppy-walking year, and her behavior should give you an idea of where we'll expect your puppies to be when they return to us."

Lenae led the group out to the van and explained how to navigate buses and seats. After she was seated and Baxter was tucked under her chair, Des went down the aisle and made sure everyone had their puppies safely out of harm's way.

"I see some bits of a chocolate Lab," he said.

Lenae felt a quick stab of guilt. She had been too distracted when Cara sat next to her, lightly pressing her leg against the length of Lenae's, to check her seatmate's puppy. Pickwick was quiet—for once—but he was the only chocolate in the class.

"His paws are under the seat," Cara protested. "You're just used to criticizing him, so you automatically do it even when he's doing something right."

"His feet are under the front of your seat, but his tail is sticking out the back." Lenae heard Des tap on the floor behind Cara with his foot.

Lenae laughed as she listened to the grunts and clipped curse words as Cara tried to get an apparently reluctant Pickwick all the way under her seat.

"Lenae, help," Cara said, but Lenae only laughed harder.

"You can't ask me to step in every time he does something wrong," she said. "I managed to fit an entire adult dog under me. Surely you can get one tiny little puppy under yours."

Cara grumbled, but after a few more moments of pushing and pulling, she got Pickwick situated well enough for Des to give his approval. "When I want him to stay still, he's like the Tasmanian Devil. When I need him to move, he flops down like he's made of cement."

"He'll learn," Lenae said, slipping easily into her soothing teacher voice. "And you'll learn. Better to struggle now and get it right than to hear a yelp of pain if someone steps on him when you're riding the bus."

Des keyed the ignition, and Lenae took advantage of the engine's noise to talk to Cara in private. "About the other day…"

"Yes?" Cara asked. Her voice sounded distracted.

"What's wrong?"

"Pickwick's hind end just rolled into the aisleway. Oof, there. He's back and Des didn't even notice."

"Yes, I did," Des said from the driver's seat.

Lenae lowered her voice even more. "As I was saying, about the other day. When I was talking about the trouble I was having with my student?"

"The one who recently lost his sight? I remember. Has he gotten any more attached to Toby?"

"No change yet," Lenae said. She was almost tempted to tell Cara about her most recent experience with Gene, when he had shown up for training class with Toby on a leash instead of in his harness. He had claimed he had forgotten and had been doing fine without it. The class was a disaster, with a confused dog and a stumbling handler. Lenae knew he was still refusing to admit his need for Toby, reluctant to let other people see this proof of his new state. She wanted to share her frustration, hear Cara's insistence that she was a good trainer, but she kept the tale to herself.

"He'll adjust soon, I'm sure," she said, not believing her own words. "But I wanted to apologize for mentioning his situation in the first place. To someone outside the center's staff. I hope you understand this is confidential—"

"And I shouldn't blab it on the news?" Cara asked. Lenae heard and felt Cara's sudden stiffening. "I can't believe you'd even feel the need to say something like that. We were talking as friends, I thought, not as part of an interview."

"I'm sorry, I didn't mean to offend you. I just wanted to be certain."

"My spots with Pickwick are just fluff pieces," Cara said. "Even if they were serious news stories, do you think anyone cares whether you're having trouble with a client?"

"Fluff pieces? Is that really all this experience means to you? All Pickwick means to you?" *All I mean to you?* Lenae didn't speak the last question out loud, but she knew it was implied by the anger in her voice.

"No," Cara said after a pause. "I apologize. Even though Pickwick drives me crazy, he really matters to me. So do…so does your center. I know you do serious work here, and I'm glad to be part of it."

"I'm sorry, too."

Cara lapsed into silence. She was angry, but mostly at herself. Her family liked to use the same phrase, and she had quoted it to Lenae with the same condescending tone her parents used. *These are little fluff pieces, but maybe they'll be enough to get you noticed. Any face time on television is good publicity.* She shuddered to herself at the bad memories.

The afternoon had been so promising. A day to herself with Pickwick and the other puppy walkers. Admittedly, she'd been especially looking forward to a chance to spend time with Lenae, minus the cameras and scripts. She had started the class with laughter, but now Lenae seemed to think she was some sort of cross between Deep Throat and Woodward and Bernstein, here to get dirt on the center and expose it on the news. She was angry with Lenae for misjudging her, but also with her parents for telling her to do almost the very thing Lenae accused her of. Fluff pieces, her dad had said, but if she could find some angle, some juicier bit of gossip than mere stories about Pickwick, then maybe she'd get more exposure, have her story picked up by the national network. The idea had made Cara sick, and Lenae's warning about privacy made her fume.

Lenae had struck a chord with Cara. Yes, Lenae had said the wrong thing, in the wrong way, but she was only voicing the things Cara already had in her head, put there by her parents and her doubts about her own worth. She wasn't sure how to get them back to the lighthearted banter they'd shared. Lenae had only been trying to protect herself, to maintain her role as authority figure and not be seen as a rookie trainer who was making mistakes, but she'd managed to offend Cara in the process. Cara had thought Lenae might be the only one who saw the real person, the person she wanted to be, behind the televised face. Now, the wall between them was a palpable thing.

They arrived downtown and gathered near Olympia's waterfront. Cara stood in the cold drizzling rain and listened while Des explained about training guide dogs to protect the handler's right shoulder. He demonstrated techniques he and Lenae were using with Gem. The puppy walkers wouldn't be teaching their charges these lessons, but after observing the upcoming aspects of training more mature dogs, Cara better understood the process as a whole and her part in it. She was fascinated in spite of her surging emotions after Lenae's hurtful comments.

Lenae stood next to her during Gem's demonstration, still in chilly silence. Cara felt the distance between them. Once Des was finished talking about Gem's stage of training, the entire class walked along the boardwalk. Des occasionally pointed out differences among the animals. Fully-trained Baxter, just-learning Gem, and the wild puppies. Cara tried to focus on his words, but her attention was on Lenae as she mingled with the class. She took Baxter to each puppy walker in turn, giving them one-on-one advice and letting Baxter act as a calming influence for each youngster.

Cara felt a mixture of relief and tension when Lenae finally directed Baxter to her.

"I'm sorry," she said as soon as Lenae was close. She paused by the railing and Lenae and Baxter stopped with her. Cara looked out over the water, at the boats gently bobbing in the harbor and the drops of rain dotting its surface. Pickwick strained at his leash and barked every time a seagull circled overhead. "I have a great deal of respect for you and the work you do at the center. I'm doing these weekly spots to promote your business, so to hear you suggest that I might do anything to compromise your clients...well, it hurt."

"You're right. I've come to realize how much integrity you have, and I shouldn't have implied you would use information I shared that way. I guess..."

Lenae's voice trailed off and she rubbed Baxter's ears with nervous-looking hands. Cara knew them both well enough by now to see the signs of Lenae's stress reflected in Baxter's more protective posture. Lenae might be able to conceal her emotions, but they were filtered through her companion in ways of which she probably wasn't aware.

"You guess...what?" Cara asked.

"I can't seem weak," Lenae admitted in a rush. "Telling you about my problems with Gene, needing and accepting your help with the center's grounds. More than anything, I need to be strong and independent. Those qualities have helped me survive so far in life, and they got me through my old job. But now, in this new place and with new responsibilities..."

For someone who had worked as one of the top newswriters in the country, Lenae seemed to be having trouble getting words out now. Cara knew what it meant for Lenae to struggle to express herself. The emotions were more difficult for her to explain than the hard facts of a news story.

"I need too many people now," Lenae continued. Cara heard her frustration. "I need Des to help me see what I can't. I need volunteers and donors. I need help managing such a large and rundown piece of property."

"And maybe you needed a friend the other day," Cara said. "Someone to listen without judging you as weak. We all need people in our lives, Lenae. You managed to get through a lot of years by creating a life that was independent, but that won't work here, with these animals and with the fallible humans who are trying to handle them. I understand what you want, to make your own way in life without relying on others, but things are different now."

Lenae reached for Cara's hand and gave it a quick squeeze. She heard the notes of something indefinable in Cara's voice, and she kept hold of her hand, keeping them connected while Cara paused.

"I've always had my family to help with my career, whether I wanted them to or not," Cara said. She traced circles on the top of Lenae's hand, and Lenae felt every cell in her skin, every tendon and blood vessel, respond to the rhythmic and whisper-soft touch. She kept her mind on Cara's words with difficulty, and she wondered if the physical touch was Cara's unconscious way of diverting attention away from what she was saying. "Some of their advice is…well, let's say they wouldn't have any qualms about using confidential information the way you thought I might. I've tried hard not to be like them, to have my own set of moral standards. When you said what you did, I heard it as an accusation that I'm just like them."

"I was only thinking of myself," Lenae admitted. She had been determined to assert her space with Cara today, prove she wasn't weak or needy, but instead she had discovered an even deeper and scarier weakness in herself. She liked Cara. Wanted to know more about her, wanted to discover the insecurities and desires that drove her. Sharing her own troubles and doubts with Cara had been dangerous. The urge to hear more about Cara's life was even more threatening to Lenae. "My business and my future. I was really rebuking myself when I said those things—because maybe I had disclosed too much—and not passing judgment on your character."

"You can talk to me without worrying that I'm secretly coming up with an eye-catching headline for your stories," Cara said. She pressed Lenae's hand with hers before letting go. "We're friends."

"Friends," Lenae repeated. She pushed away from the railing and walked back to the van with Cara and Pickwick. After a vigorous shake, all the puppies settled quietly under their seats. Fresh air and the long walk had made even Gem and Baxter ready for a nap. Lenae and Cara were quiet, too, on the way back to the center, but with none of the defensive walls between them, as there'd been on the way to town. Friendship, sharing, vulnerability. Lenae had tried to experience those in her past but had been used. Her weakness had been used against her. Could she trust Cara enough to let down her guard again? Lenae wasn't sure, and she wasn't in a hurry to find out and possibly— probably—get hurt again.

CHAPTER FIFTEEN

Lenae took a seat near the front of the bus and felt Baxter wedge himself underneath her. Out of habit, she checked to make sure his paws were safely tucked out of harm's way. She chatted quietly with him as they rode, telling him they were on their way to meet Cara and Pickwick for their one-month evaluation. She wasn't sure he'd be able to hear her over the roar of the diesel engine, but at the mention of Cara's name he raised his head and licked her hand. Maybe he was excited to see Cara—he always responded to her name or presence with more excitement than Lenae was accustomed to seeing in her serious dog. He even seemed to enjoy the antics of Pickwick, although he'd never seemed particularly fond of wild puppies.

On the other hand, maybe Baxter was trying to comfort her with his wet nose and rasping tongue. She was unaccountably nervous about seeing Cara again. Their conversations had been growing increasingly personal, and even though Lenae was coming to appreciate having Cara as a friend, her old habits of privacy and recalcitrance were difficult to overcome. She couldn't help but worry that secrets told in confidence might come back to haunt her someday. She'd become preoccupied with Cara's revelations as well. There was something touching about Cara. She seemed successful in the media world, unsurprising given her breeding, but she was more in touch with her inner self than Lenae had expected. An entire family of actors. Lenae had lived with one fame-hungry woman, and had worked among countless others, but she couldn't imagine growing up in a home full of people so adept at putting on an outward show. Had Cara been nurtured as a child, or prepped for the cameras?

Despite her growing interest in Cara's life and upbringing, they weren't strictly Lenae's business except where Pickwick was concerned. And Cara had surprised Lenae in that regard also. She was taking the puppy-walking job seriously, and applying everything Lenae taught her with diligence. At first, Lenae had thought she might be working hard only so she looked good on the news spots, but now she knew better. Knew Cara and her motives a little better. Cara hadn't brought the cameras along when she came to the center with her students, or the day of the class field trip to Olympia. Instead, the trip had been a time of quiet revelations for them both. And the day with Cara's students had been a peaceful one with undocumented work and friendly kids. The dogs at the center had loved the attention of the college students, and Lenae had been left with patched fences, an aerated and seeded lawn, and the enticing scent of herbs from Cara's hanging basket. Rosemary for remembrance. Lenae couldn't walk through the office door without plucking off a leaf and letting the smell bring her day with Cara vividly back to mind.

A friendship was nice, but Lenae couldn't be sidetracked by Cara. She had her five-year plan for establishing her business, and Cara had other career goals to follow. Lenae had wanted out of the fast-paced news world, especially since she had lost faith in her ability to discern truth from self-serving fiction. Cara was on the edge of the limelight, but about to be pushed farther in. Lenae knew the qualities of timbre and voice control necessary for success in the television medium, and Cara had those in abundance. And according to everything Lenae had read or heard, Cara had the gorgeous looks to back them up. No, whether that was Cara's ambition or not, she was going places, and Lenae wouldn't ever again be collateral damage to someone else's career move.

Baxter seemed to sense when they had neared their stop, although she had never taken him to Evergreen College before. She took hold of his harness and got to her feet when the driver opened the doors. Although her puppy-walking sessions were held at the center or on group trips around the area, she wanted to get in the habit of visiting her volunteers in their own environments as well. Too much time with Cara might not be in her best interests—since even her logical awareness of their different career paths couldn't make her attraction to Cara disappear—but at least the privacy-denying presence of the news cameras would help her keep an emotional distance.

"Hi, Lenae. Hey, Baxter." Cara greeted them when they stepped off the bus. The heavy diesel fumes couldn't quite hide the scent of fir and damp ground, and Lenae felt as if the forest was encroaching on them where they stood.

"Hello, Cara. And hello to you, Pickwick. You're being very polite today." The puppy had jumped on her once but had responded to Cara's quiet command of *off*. Lenae bent down to scratch his ears. He wasn't sitting, but he was politely standing by her side. When she straightened up again, she felt him leap up to bite Baxter's neck.

"Sorry. He can only be good for so long," Cara said with a sigh. "Pickwick, leave poor Baxter alone!"

Lenae laughed. "He's improving, so focus on the good and don't worry about what's going wrong. Concentrate on being consistent, and eventually his emotional growth will catch up. One day he'll surprise you with how much he was learning even though he was too young to follow the lessons."

"Again, I'll have to take your word for it. In the meantime, all the chairs and tables in my house are a few inches shorter because he's been gnawing on the legs."

Lenae put her hand on Cara's shoulder and kneaded the tight muscles she felt there. Cara joked about her puppy issues, but Lenae understood the truth behind the humor. Cara was devoting plenty of time and energy to Pickwick, and therefore to Lenae's center. She wanted to continue massaging Cara's tension away, as much for her own pleasure since she loved the quiet moans Cara made under her touch, but she couldn't forget they were standing in the middle of a busy campus. "Maybe we should let him have a good run with Baxter before the film crew gets here, so he won't be distracting while you shoot the news spot. Is there a safe place for him to be loose around here?"

"The crew isn't coming today. Did you want them here? I thought we could take the dogs down to Eld Inlet and let them play on the beach."

Because I'm sick of having my every move recorded. Because I'd like to spend time with you. Cara didn't add those reasons to her list. "I thought it'd be easier to talk about Pickwick's training without worrying about being filmed."

"Oh, of course. I'm sure Baxter will enjoy a hike to the water. He loves to swim."

Cara led the way across the campus, but she stopped at the communications building. "This is where I work. It's basically a big concrete rectangle, but it has some interesting reddish and glass shapes on the roof. All the buildings are very spartan and defined, from the outside."

"They must look interesting set here in a forest. Hard materials and forms, growing out of the softer insistence of the woods around them. Can we go into your office?"

"Sure." Cara covered her surprise by going over to a tree to rescue Pickwick from a tangled leash. She hadn't expected Lenae to want to visit her personal space, or to be able to understand the visual interest Cara had in the college campus. She was constantly surprising her. Cara held the door of the building open for Lenae and Baxter, telling Lenae about the posters and displays as they walked down the hall. Some of the fine arts students had photographs hanging on the walls, and Lenae paused by each one as Cara described it.

When Lenae had finished asking questions about the photographs, they continued down the hall. Cara debated mentally about asking a question of her own, and she finally gave in to her curiosity.

"You seem to grasp the concepts of what makes a photo artistic. I didn't expect the subject to interest you since photography's strictly a visual medium."

Lenae paused before she answered, but Cara had a feeling she was trying to frame her answer, not that she was offended by the question.

"I understand composition. Everywhere I go, every time I enter a room, I have to orient myself to doors and furniture and people. So even though I can't see photos or paintings, I can imagine the spatial relations between the objects in them. I also get the interplay of sun and shadow—not visually like you, but in the sense of warmth and cold. I experience the artwork in different ways than a sighted person, but the subject matter can still have the ability to affect me."

"I suppose it's the same with any artistic form," Cara said as they walked. Lenae had rested her hand on Cara's forearm for guidance and Cara slid her own hand over it, gently fitting her fingers between Lenae's. "Say we both read a poem. The imagery and ideas in it will affect me in a certain way because of my past and my state of mind, but you might read something entirely different into it. The power of the artist to affect and change us is the constant."

Lenae squeezed Cara's fingers softly. "Most people aren't able to get past their disbelief when I say I enjoy the visual arts," she said. "You focused on what makes us similar, not what makes us unlike each other."

"We have unique ways of encountering what our senses perceive, but we're doing the same thing at heart. Trying to make sense of the world around us and to understand our place in it. And as for my place in the universe," Cara injected a wry note, "this, such as it is, is my office."

"You sound almost apologetic," Lenae said with a laugh. "I'll take that to mean it's a mess in here?"

Cara was about to protest, but she had to laugh as well. Her first instinct, when they had come through the door and until she reminded herself that Lenae couldn't see the clutter, had been to start tidying up. She should have expected Lenae to know it wasn't neat even without being able to see the haphazard stacks, especially since she'd visited Cara's home and knew her housekeeping habits, or lack thereof. "Maybe, a little. It didn't help when I had to take all the books and papers off the floor so Pickwick wouldn't destroy them."

"Are you blaming the innocent puppy for your bad habits?" Lenae touched the edge of the desk and followed it until she reached Cara's chair. She sat down and unsnapped Baxter's lead. He went over to Pickwick's unused cushion and curled up for a nap.

"Innocent isn't the word I'd use to describe the little hellion, but I'll admit I'm a slob."

"You'd drive me crazy," Lenae said as she ran her hand over the objects on the desk. "I have to have everything in place."

"I could change," Cara said. Why had she spoken the words out loud? "I mean, I've had to change, for Pickwick. I don't think being messy is part of who I am, so I've been able to make adjustments."

Lenae touched papers and books and a couple of empty coffee cups before she found a small clay object. She picked it up and ran her fingers over it, searching for some identifying clue, trying to distract her mind from contemplating Cara's original statement. It had sounded personal until she'd attempted to explain it away. Lenae didn't want to even think about Cara in her space, in her home. But she wouldn't mind a few bumps and bruises if Cara wasn't as obsessively neat as she was. "Part of being a pet owner is making changes," she said, following Cara's change in subject. "Just like having a child. Speaking of children, did one make this for you or were you a kid when you made it?"

"I did. I was in first grade. Can you tell what it is?"

Lenae turned the object around in her hands. "There's a small indentation on either side, so I'd guess it's an ashtray. The paint is bumpy on this side, so you wrote someone's name over the background color. Is this a *D*? Yes, you made this for your dad." Lenae stopped talking but kept following the clues. Cara's dad was very much alive and delivering the sports scores on television every night. The only reason she could find for Cara to still have the primitive piece of art was because her father didn't want it. What kind of parent would reject a child's offering?

"Very good," Cara said. She took the ashtray from Lenae's hands. "But I made the indentations too small. My dad smoked cigars and not cigarettes."

Lenae had no idea how to respond to Cara's flatly delivered comment. She heard the pain in Cara's voice as clearly as if she'd announced it in words. What made Cara keep this reminder of a childhood hurt so close at hand? "He should have taken up cigarettes," she said.

Cara set the ashtray back on her desk with a loud clunk. "Thank you. I've known that, of course, but I've never been able to actually say it out loud. What parent wouldn't make a fuss over a child's gift, even if it wasn't useful or particularly beautiful? I've kept that damned thing with me for years, moving it from desk to desk whenever I changed jobs, always there as a reminder. Of what? The ability to rise above disappointment? The foolishness of expecting kindness or allowances? Or, better yet, it was probably my first lesson in the importance—or is triviality the right word?— of appearances. Love doesn't matter, but form does."

Lenae cleared her throat and felt for other objects on the desk. She had noticed too much when she'd felt the memento of Cara's childhood, and she searched for a way to lighten the suddenly closed atmosphere in the small room. Books, papers, thick file folders. Nothing specific to give her a new topic, but the generalities might work to get Cara's mind off the past. "What classes are you teaching this semester?"

"Just one, but I'm the lead professor for it, so it's very time-consuming. It's called Rooted in Place, and it's about the definitions and influences that make us the people we are. We'll do classwork and also make a student-produced film about each student's self-defined roots."

Not exactly the change in subject Lenae had anticipated. She marveled at Cara's desire to keep focused on her past and her own roots even though they seemed to cause her pain. "It sounds interesting. Will you have a part in the film?"

"I'm not sure," Cara said. Lenae heard the rasp of clay on wood and wondered if Cara was still toying with the ashtray. "I might do a short spot on my family and what it was like being raised in the media."

"I'm sure it had plenty of challenges." Lenae stopped exploring Cara's desk with her hand and instead scratched Baxter's ears. "Different expectations and experiences."

"Different values…" Cara's voice faltered to a halt. She cleared her throat and started again. "Since you're interested in composition and visual arts, how would you produce the story of your own life for film? It's going to be a challenge for my students to decide what is important enough to include and what's not as significant."

Lenae sat quietly for a moment, piecing together childhood memories into a coherent sequence. She had been most wounded and changed by her recent betrayal, but she didn't want to talk about that with Cara. So she stuck to her early years.

"I think my story would best be told by responses to events, not the events themselves," she said, groping for the right words to express what she meant. "Most people believe I'm defined by my disability, but what really defines me is how I react to it. My mom played a big part in that. So my story wouldn't be about the burned hands when I tried to cook or my cut knee when I fell off the neighbor kid's bike. It'd be about the way Mom had me brainstorm ways to make it safe and possible for me to cook or ride a bike. She helped at first, but I took those lessons with me to college and to work."

"You ride bikes?" Cara asked, hating the note of disbelief in her question. Lenae only laughed, her expression at ease as if she wasn't offended by Cara's curiosity.

"Unless I'm very confident in my surroundings, I stick to the back seat of tandem bikes. But I used to ride around the track after school, and Mom and I would ride around the block together. She had a bell on her handlebars so I knew where she was and stayed close behind."

"You're amazing," Cara said before she could stop herself. She knew bike riding wasn't inspirational—people did it every day—and she hoped Lenae understood that she wasn't praising her for living a full life. No, she gave people plenty of compliments when interviewing them, but this feeling she had for Lenae was different. Lenae had learned about Cara's deficient past, about her parents who wanted to mold her in their image, to limit her scope. And *she* had learned about Lenae's mother, who had opened the world to her daughter and raised her to be confident and strong in her own abilities. And Lenae was confident and strong, much stronger than Cara feared she was herself.

"I think you are, too," Lenae said quietly.

Cara couldn't conceal her reflexive scoff at Lenae's comment. "An amazing potter? Or an amazing organizer? Certainly not an amazing puppy trainer."

"I'm not joking," Lenae said. "You're much better with Pickwick than you give yourself credit for, but that's not what I meant. You're amazing because of the honest way you explore yourself and your past. And instead of only using what you learn for your own benefit, you share your knowledge with others. With your students and audience. And with me, like you did when we were talking about the photos in the hall."

Cara wrapped Pickwick's lead around her wrist. Lenae seemed serious, but Cara couldn't come up with a response that didn't sound unappreciative or disbelieving. She shifted the attention off herself and onto the dogs. "Shall we take these two out for a hike now?"

"Yes," Lenae agreed after a brief pause. She stood up and grasped Baxter's harness. "Let's go to the beach."

CHAPTER SIXTEEN

O ops, I'm sorry. I didn't notice the root back there." Cara had suggested they let Baxter be off duty while they followed the path through the woods and down to the beach, but she hadn't realized how varied the terrain really was. She had been along this same route many times, and it seemed to be a straightforward trip. When she was responsible for being another person's eyes, she suddenly began to notice every dip and rock and bend in the trail.

"It's okay. I'm fine," Lenae said. Her hand rested on Cara's elbow as they walked. "Makes you realize how much Baxter does for me, doesn't it?"

Cara watched Baxter and Pickwick as they alternately strained at the leashes and stopped to sniff plants and stumps along the way. She admired Baxter for what he offered Lenae and for how happily and well he did his job. She couldn't imagine Pickwick doing the same thing for his future owner. She had a vision of him dragging some pour soul along a forest trail, like a person in a pinball machine, bouncing off trees and boulders and waterskiing over streams.

"Why are you laughing?" Lenae asked. "Does my twisted ankle amuse you?"

Cara bumped Lenae with her shoulder. "No, of course not. Careful here, we need to step over a log." She slowed down and guided Lenae over the obstacle. "I was laughing because I was imagining Pickwick in harness. I can see, and he gets me into trouble when we walk down an empty sidewalk."

"You have no imagination," Lenae said. She ran into a low-hanging branch and took hold of it, using it to swat playfully at Cara. "Look at what a terrible guide dog you are right now. But I believe in you, and with the correct training methods I believe I'll be able to whip you into shape."

Cara took Lenae's hand and moved it from her elbow to her shoulder. "The path narrows here, so it'll be difficult to walk side-by-side. I'll sacrifice my pretty face and blaze a trail for you through all these branches. What training methods did you have in mind? Extra treats to reward good behavior?" Was the whipping a threat or a promise?

Lenae rested both hands on Cara's shoulders. Although she had fought against being seen as disabled with a guide dog when she first got Baxter, now she rarely relinquished the independence and freedom he gave her. Her restricted movement seemed even more pronounced to her when directly compared to her guided pace and mobility. But she wouldn't have missed this trek for the world. She would have had an easier trip with Baxter guiding her, but she was enjoying the rare, desirable human contact with Cara enough to struggle through whatever stubborn self-consciousness she still carried with her. Even if Cara had been leading her flawlessly, Lenae might have been too distracted to follow her without tripping over her own feet. "Treats work in some cases, but with you I was thinking a mild electric shock every time you make a mistake…"

Cara halted abruptly and Lenae bumped into her. "Do I need to report you to some sort of human rights organization?"

Lenae's body was flush against Cara's back, but she didn't move away. "All right, no shocks. But maybe one of those pronged training collars around your neck." Lenae lifted her hands off Cara's shoulders and lightly encircled her neck. "Just to keep you from misbehaving."

Cara took Lenae's hands and firmly put them back on her own shoulders. "Keep touching me like that, and I'll do plenty of misbehaving." She cleared her throat. "We're going down to the beach now. The trail is going to be steep, so I'll go slowly."

"Maybe I should let the expert take over now," Lenae said. She let go of Cara's shoulders and called Baxter to her. She had been all too aware of her physical reaction to Cara's nearness, but this was the first time she'd had a hint that Cara noticed an attraction, too. She wasn't sure how to process the information yet, especially on a tricky mountain trail, so she retreated to the comfort of Baxter's guidance.

Cara watched the dog shift into his careful, protective mode. He stayed close to Lenae and helped her down the slope. She seemed to read his thoughts as she followed his lead. Cara concentrated on getting herself down the hill without being dragged off the cliff by Pickwick, but she felt the loss of Lenae's touch. She'd dated plenty of women in the past—of course, never quite sure if she was the attraction, or her famous family—but no one's touch had affected her like this. How easy to let her façade slip when she was distracted by the feelings stirring from her shoulders, where Lenae's hands had been, directly to her belly. And once she was free of her barriers, Lenae would realize Cara's big secret. That there wasn't anything beyond the face.

Perversely, she wanted to hide the truth about herself and get it out in the open at the same time. She felt as vulnerable as she had when Lenae had picked up the ashtray and read it through her fingers, as if she was reading a page of braille. Cara's insecurities, her fears—constantly reinforced by her parents—that she would never measure up to the expectations of her family. Lenae noticed too much, and Cara needed distance. She wanted to push Lenae away, and Pickwick gave her the opportunity. If anything would make Lenae keep her distance, it would be the thought of Cara using her puppy walking for selfish reasons. "I have to remember to thank Des for choosing Pickwick for me," she said, picking up the squirming puppy and attempting to carry him for a few yards.

"He might not be the most successful guide dog, but he has one special skill."

"What's that?"

"He's a chick magnet. I can't walk through the store without being stopped at least once per department. Whatever else happens this year, I won't be hurting for dates."

Cara saw Lenae's back stiffen, but she didn't respond. If Lenae had had any doubts about Cara's shallowness or about her less-than-ideal motives for puppy walking, Cara had just managed to prove her right. She wasn't lying about Pickwick's ability to attract women, but she neglected to mention her own lack of interest in the women who wanted to talk to her about Pickwick. Most of them mentioned the news spots, and Cara knew the combination of her family name and looks, combined with Pickwick's puppy charm, was irresistible. Both attracted attention, but not for the right reasons.

Lenae relaxed once the walk from the bluff to the beach was over. The path had been tricky, with snags and a constant decline, but worse had been Cara's admission about meeting other women. Lenae had been having fun, sharing her comments about the photos and learning about Cara by visiting her office, but somehow the thought of Cara dating other women made her feel sick. By now, she knew without a doubt that Cara was joking about using Pickwick in any way, but she didn't have to work hard to imagine women stumbling over themselves to talk to Cara. Of course, she'd never date Cara, she wasn't her type, they were too different, and…

Lenae sighed. Who was she kidding? She had gone over and over the reasons why she and Cara had no business developing a personal relationship beyond friendship. Her illogical response merely told her that she was more attracted to Cara than she had thought. Her hurt feelings had nothing to do with Cara's actions and everything to do with her own runaway attraction. She could control one, but not the other.

❖

"Do you mind if I let Baxter run?" Lenae asked when they reached the beach. It meant she'd need to touch Cara again, but she couldn't deny her dog a bout of freedom. "He loves the beach, and we don't get to the water often enough."

"Sure." Cara said. "He and Pickwick can play in the surf while we walk. I thought we could visit the college's marine biology lab, and I can introduce you to a friend of mine."

Lenae unhooked Baxter's harness, and then slipped her arm through Cara's. She breathed deeply, loving the salty air filling her lungs. The murky and fishy scent of low tide, the call of gulls overhead, the breeze lifting her hair and caressing the back of her neck. She needed this walk on the beach as much as Baxter did.

"I've never been to this part of Puget Sound," Lenae said, distracting herself from the warmth of Cara's skin, softly moist from the exertion of their hike, under her palm. "Will you describe it for me?"

"We're at low tide right now, so the beach is covered with seaweed and broken shells. There are tall evergreen trees along the cliff behind us, and across the inlet, so it almost seems like we're enclosed. You can see some houses on the other side of the water, the city of Olympia is just over the hill, and the college is right behind us, but it feels like we're...I don't know..."

Cara's speech slowed to a halt.

"In a terrarium?" Lenae asked.

Cara sighed. "Yes. That's a good way to describe it. Isolated and self-contained."

"I can sense an echo, almost," Lenae said. She turned her head into the breeze coming off the water and closed her eyes. "As if we're surrounded by stone and forest. But I can smell the chill of the ocean in the wind. No matter how separate some of these inlets are, they're still connected to the Pacific. Part of it. Ocean air fills my lungs like no other air can."

Cara swallowed and turned away from the gorgeous sight of Lenae's face. Peace and relaxation softened her often somber appearance. She had the ability to fully immerse herself in an environment in a way Cara—so dependent on her sight—was unable to do. She watched Pickwick and Baxter take turns chasing each other through the wet sand. Baxter waded into the water until the long golden hairs on his belly touched the surface.

"The dogs are going to be muddy messes," Cara said as Pickwick trotted toward them with a strand of kelp in his mouth, most of it dragging behind him. "Maybe Tess will have some towels so we can clean them before we head back."

Cara had spent many lunch hours down here once she had met Tess, the head of the marine biology department, but she hadn't yet brought Pickwick to meet her friend. She and Tess had noticed each other immediately at Cara's first faculty get-together. She thought Tess was attractive, of course, with her athletic body and killer legs, but they were too different to even consider dating. Tess had a long list of requirements her potential partners had to meet, and Cara failed the test since she taught at the college and was looking for a relationship that would last longer than an afternoon. But she had found a sense of validation from Tess and their friendship. To have a smart and funny woman seek her out for companionship made Cara feel good, and the moment Lenae had told her she was coming to the college for Pickwick's evaluation, Cara had known she wanted the two to meet.

Cara saw Tess pulling a sailboat onto the shore a few hundred yards ahead, where she was boisterously greeted by the two dogs. Tess shaded her eyes with her hand and turned toward Cara and Lenae. Even at such a long distance, Cara could see the admiration in Tess's eyes when she looked at Lenae. Perhaps her decision to bring Lenae here had been rash. She had wanted Lenae to meet her friend, maybe to prove there was something worthy in her, but that was before Lenae had read her ashtray like tea leaves and seen too much. But the thought of the two of them hitting it off made her feel a bit queasy. And that made no sense at all.

"Hey, Cara! Is this your puppy? And who's this handsome fellow?" Tess quickly covered the distance between them, the two dogs cavorting in her wake.

"Hi, Tess. Meet Pickwick and Baxter. And this is Lenae, the guide-dog trainer. Lenae, this is Tess Hansen, the Northwest's leading expert on orcas in Puget Sound." Cara kept Lenae's hand tucked in the crook of her arm, but Lenae tugged loose and reached toward Tess.

"It's nice to meet you, Tess. I'm fascinated by whales and their songs. What an interesting area of study." Lenae shook hands with Tess, and Cara wanted to pull the two of them apart. She hadn't thought this through. Yes, she wanted to push Lenae away, to put some distance between them, but she wasn't ready to push her all the way into Tess's arms. Her front-row view of Tess's smile when she looked at Lenae made for an uncomfortable walk to the biology lab.

"I have some recordings of the pod I've been studying," Tess said.

"I'd love to hear them." Lenae called Baxter and he immediately trotted to her side. Pickwick had flushed a seagull, so he ignored Cara's whistle and ran farther down the beach.

"What next, are you going to offer to show her your etchings?" Cara mumbled as she jogged after her puppy. He wasn't ready to give up the chase after his seagull, and her jeans and shoes were soaked from the wet sand by the time she caught him. She carried him back to the lab, his scrabbling paws leaving dirty tracks on her gray T-shirt, to find Lenae sitting near a tiny space heater with Baxter at her feet.

"Cara?" Lenae called when the door clicked shut. Pickwick's nails tapped across the floor toward her. "Was Pickwick enjoying his run on the beach too much to be caught?"

"Yes." Cara said shortly.

"Here, feel this, Lenae," Tess said. Lenae held out her hands and took the object from her. "There you are, Cara. Thought we lost you out there."

Lenae slid her hand over the arced bone in her hand, curving her fingers over the jagged teeth. "Amazing," she said. "I hadn't realized how large their teeth are."

"I have some other marine mammal skulls here. Let me get a few more for you to compare with this one, plus I have a leftover sandwich from lunch for Baxter. Oh, and your puppy can have some, too, Cara."

"Your friend is nice," Lenae said when they were alone. Cara had been uncommonly quiet since they had arrived on the beach, but every time she spoke, her voice had an edge to it.

"Yes, Tess is great. But be careful. She's as predatory as those killer whales she studies."

Lenae laughed at Cara's warning. She thought Tess seemed friendly, but she hadn't thought anything of it until Cara made her comment. Maybe that explained her subdued mood. Was Cara jealous? Of her, or of Tess?

"Is she one of the chicks you're trying to attract with Pickwick?"

"No! She's a good friend, but there's nothing between us. We work together, and besides, we want totally different things out of a relationship. I'm just trying to protect you from taking her too seriously."

"Ah. You're trying to protect poor innocent little me," Lenae said with a laugh. "I thought you had too much to worry about with all the women fawning over you and Pickwick to care about *my* romantic life."

"Don't look so smug. She'd flirt with one of the pylons outside if she thought she had a chance of getting it to go home with her."

Tess returned with a porpoise skull and half of a tuna-fish sandwich for Baxter before she went off to another part of the lab to find more treasures for Lenae. Baxter wolfed down the treat without bothering to chew it.

"She's like a dog playing fetch," Cara said.

Lenae only laughed harder. "I guess Pickwick isn't the only chick magnet around here," she said. "Baxter seems to be holding his own."

Cara was working on a smart retort when Tess came back with a couple of towels and a portable CD player. She tossed the towels at Cara.

"Your shirt is all muddy," Tess said. She knelt and Pickwick ran over to her. "Here you go, cutie," she said, giving him a cookie.

"It's cutie's fault that I'm such a mess." She wiped at the paw prints covering the front of her shirt but only managed to smear the dirt around.

"Lenae, I thought you might want to hear some recordings I made of J pod when I was studying them last summer." She pushed play and the eerily beautiful music of the whales filled the small room. Cara watched Lenae listen—her face rapt as her fingers traced the outline of the porpoise skull she still held in her hands. Tess paused the recording a few times to identify specific whales in the pod, and after a few minutes, Lenae was able to pick each distinctive voice out of the crowd, commenting on the qualities of each whale's song.

This from a woman who couldn't carry a tune when she was singing with the radio.

Cara sat on the floor near the heater and pulled a resisting Pickwick onto her lap. She rubbed his muddy paws with the towel, succeeding in getting it filthy without seeming to make much difference in Pickwick's level of cleanliness. She gave up and let him loose to snuffle around Baxter, licking up the occasional sandwich crumb. Whale songs and baleen and shark teeth. Tess had an arsenal of interesting objects for Lenae to touch or listen to. Cara had only had an old ashtray, a relic from her odd childhood. She couldn't compete with Tess. Besides, hadn't she already alienated Lenae by telling her about Pickwick's magnetic personality? She leaned back on one hand and pulled her vibrating phone out of her pocket. She saw her dad's name and sighed. He was probably calling to give her more tips for improving her performance on his news show. She had received similar calls every week and was tempted to ignore this one, but even talking to her dad seemed preferable to listening to Tess and Lenae discuss whales.

"Hey, Dad," she said, turning away from Lenae as Tess handed her another handful of bones. What a creepy way to flirt.

"Great news, child. Your weekly spot has gotten some special notice."

"Well, good. Hopefully it'll mean more donations and support for Lenae's center." Lenae turned in her direction and Baxter perked up his ears at the sound of her name.

"Oh, yes…of course," Howard continued. "I'm sure it will. Because you and that puppy of yours are going to be on national television, and she's invited to be there, too."

"What?" Cara's voice must have revealed her dismay because even Tess and Pickwick stopped what they were doing and looked at her.

"What's wrong?" Lenae asked. "Is it bad news?"

"Depends on your interpretation." Cara hesitated to explain because she was quite certain Lenae would be less than thrilled by the news. "We have to go home and pack because our flight leaves in the morning."

"Flight? To where? Why?" Lenae handed the bones back to Tess and stood. Baxter moved close to her side.

"To New York," Cara said miserably. "We're going to be on the *Morning Across America* show in two days."

CHAPTER SEVENTEEN

Lenae felt along the edge of the airplane aisle to make sure Baxter's paws and tail were safe from being trodden on when the rest of the passengers boarded. She sat back in her seat with a sigh. The normal pre-boarding period was usually more than enough time for her and Baxter, but the additional responsibility of Cara and Pickwick had meant every second was needed to get settled. She'd have preferred not to be on the flight at all, but at least Cara's dad had insisted on buying them first-class tickets. Trying to maneuver through the coach section with a manic puppy, his nervous handler, and all the well-intentioned but annoying attendants would have been too much for Lenae to handle.

She kicked off her shoes and tucked her feet under the blanket she had brought for the dogs to lie on, since the floor could get cold during the flight. She burrowed her toes beneath the comforting weight of Baxter and wondered when the drink cart would begin its trek down the aisle. She pulled out her earbuds and felt for the port on her armrest.

"Pickwick, stop that!" Cara said for the hundredth time since they had boarded. Lenae sighed again. It was going to be a long five hours.

"What's he doing wrong?" she asked. So far, she had been impressed by Pickwick's behavior. He had been curious but not afraid as they had gone through the long process of security checks and waiting at the gate and boarding. Sea-Tac had been crowded, of course, but he had seemed unfazed by the new experience. Exactly what she'd hope for from a guide-dog candidate. Cara, on the other hand, might need a sedative.

"He keeps jumping up to look out the window."

"So, let him. He'll get bored soon and settle down. This has been a busy morning for him, and he'll probably sleep most of the flight." Lenae hoped Cara might do the same thing. She had been tense and irritable since her father's call the day before. Lenae assumed it was because she was nervous about performing well on tomorrow's show, but she didn't believe there was any cause for concern. Cara came alive when she was being filmed. Everything about her was bright and beautiful, and tomorrow the whole nation would have a chance to witness her transformation. She'd be a success.

Lenae put her hand on Cara's forearm and moved until she found Cara's hand. "You'll be great. Don't worry. Are you shredding your boarding pass?"

Cara looked at her lap and saw the bits of paper. "Yes. Luckily we don't have a connecting flight." She turned her hand over and interlaced her fingers with Lenae's. Pickwick put his forepaws on her knees and looked at her with his usual unperturbed puppy grin, as if he couldn't believe what an adventure they were having. "And I'm not worried. I just don't want to do this."

All right, part of her *did* want to do the morning show. Part of her was thrilled because she had been noticed, had gotten approval. Had been asked to fly across the country and appear on national television. But those parts were the ones she had fought against her whole life. She did her public television show because she wanted to raise awareness of people who were doing good in the world. How had one segment about a guide-dog center turned into a promotional campaign for her own career? And she *liked* it. What further proof did she need that she had no more genuine depth than anyone else in her family?

Cara squeezed Lenae's hand and then pulled away to stop Pickwick as he tried to crawl under the seat in front of her. Lenae hadn't wanted to be here, but Cara had dragged her along. She had debated with her for over an hour about the merits of being on the show and doing a short demonstration with Baxter. Lenae had argued she needed local exposure, but not necessarily national. She had been less able to refute Cara's claim that the show would be a great addition to any grant application. But Cara's main reason for insisting she come was because she couldn't imagine flying alone with Pickwick, without Lenae's unruffled help and logic. Lenae had been calm and unbothered by the ordeal of traveling with Pickwick, and Cara was amazed by her ability to remain serene not just when dealing with the details of flying with dogs in tow, but despite all the humans along the way.

Cara hadn't fully appreciated before this what life was like for Lenae. There were people who tried to help and guide her by grabbing her arm and dragging her along. Some spoke slowly to her as if she wasn't a highly intelligent and capable woman, while others shouted as if she was hard of hearing. Even worse were the ones who addressed their comments to Cara, ignoring Lenae completely. Cara wanted to slap the attendant who came by and reached for Lenae's seat belt, explaining in excruciating detail how to adjust the straps.

"How do you stand it?" she asked when the flight attendant left, turning the conversation away from her pitiful bid for media attention and onto Lenae.

"I just keep reminding myself you have a big performance tomorrow, and you're usually not this annoying."

"Ha-ha. You know what I meant. And I'm not being annoying."

"That's a matter of opinion," Lenae said with a smile. She patted Cara's knee. "I do know what you mean. I've lived with this sort of unwelcome help my entire life, from people who don't seem to recognize me as a functioning human being. It's part of my life—not a good part, but not something that will change anytime soon. It's easy to notice the boorish or ignorant attitudes, but if you really pay attention you'll find there are people who are much more respectful and thoughtful. The small gestures, like the woman who checked our boarding passes at the gate and arranged for our bags to be stowed for us, or the man at the ticket counter who called ahead to the gate so they'd be ready for us. Those can be overlooked if you only concentrate on the obnoxious people."

Cara shook her head. She wasn't convinced she'd be able to have such a good outlook if she were in Lenae's place. "I hate having people do things for me. Favors I don't want, but then am expected to repay. Ulterior motives. Like my dad pushing for me to do the news show and now this morning show."

"Two different worlds," Lenae said. "Most of the people who are too intrusive when they help me are genuinely trying to do something good, although sometimes I'm sure they want to look admirable by having others see them assisting the poor blind woman. But in showbiz, you're expected to have the attitude of reciprocity. You scratch my back—"

"I'll scratch your eyes out."

Lenae laughed, but it sounded more cynical than humorous. "Been there. Three-N was notorious for backstabbing and information leaks."

"Is that why you left?"

Lenae leaned closer to Cara as the crowd of boarders pushed into her space. She put her leg protectively between Baxter and the aisle. "One incident in particular," she said. Too private to share. "But you're doing fine on your own. You have *Around the Sound* and your teaching job. Your father might have prompted these new opportunities, but for the most part you're making it on your own."

Lenae heard Cara's breathing change its rhythm. "Actually, I'm not. The show hardly pays anything, and I only teach part-time. I use the money I inherited from my grandmother to support myself in those two careers. So I'm still cashing in on the Bradley name, even if I'm not featured nightly on some high-profile show." Was that *shame* Lenae heard in Cara's voice? In this strong, talented, generous woman's admission that she wasn't entirely independent?

"What's wrong with that? She left the money to you, and you're using it in a way that helps a lot of people. I researched your show before I agreed to do the segment, and you've brought some great organizations and individuals much-needed publicity. And you're sharing your knowledge with students at a college focused on community and the environment. There's nothing to be ashamed of. You should be proud of what you do. Look at my center—I can't keep it open without financial help from foundations and philanthropists. Does that mean I'm not doing something important, just because I'm not paying for it myself?"

"Of course not. But it's different. You're actively improving the life of every person who gets one of your dogs. I'm just a pretty mouthpiece for some charities."

Lenae wondered at Cara's use of the word *pretty*. She spit it out as if it was something vile. Beauty was obviously not simple for Cara, nor was her relationship with her family. Complex and personal. Lenae should stay out of Cara's business, but she knew what Cara did when the cameras weren't watching her. She devoted her time to Pickwick and her students, she made baskets of herbs and organized groups of volunteer gardeners and painters. Even when she could have brought cameras along to document her good deeds, she chose instead to do them quietly. "Not true. You're making the world better in your own way, using your unique talents and assets. And you're giving your time and energy to puppy walk Pickwick. Even though it started as a stunt for the news spot, you're still doing something useful and worthwhile. And doing it very well."

"Not really," Cara said. "He's been chewing on your briefcase handle while we've been talking. I didn't say anything because for once he was being quiet."

Lenae reached for her briefcase and pulled it away from Pickwick's determined jaws. She took two bones out of the case and gave one to each dog. "Well, you *usually* do a good job with him. I'll let this time slide because it's been a tiring day." The plane's engines started up and Pickwick whined softly. Lenae felt Cara stiffen beside her and she distracted her with questions.

"When did you start performing? Was it something your family encouraged, or something you chose to do?"

Cara reached under her seat and found the bone Pickwick had dropped. She gave it back to him and was relieved when he took it without fuss, seemingly adapting to the whine of the engines. "I wouldn't say there was much choice in it. I was on-screen before I could walk. Anytime there was a casting call, I'd be there with my mom or the nanny, in pigtails and frilly dresses or baby designer jeans and a tiny baseball hat—whatever the required dress was for the part. My parents knew how to play the game and how to present me for parts, so I got plenty of work as a child."

"I'm sure you had more to do with getting roles than you realized," Lenae said.

"Because I was pretty? That helped, but the family connections counted even more than looks. I didn't understand most of my lines, and I often didn't even know what I was supposed to be selling, but I knew one thing. My parents were proud of me when I got a part, we'd all go out to dinner together, and they'd talk to me about the role and run lines with me. I was thrilled when I was cast and devastated when I wasn't."

"What were they like when you weren't playing a part?" Lenae reached for Cara's hand.

Cara traced her fingers over Lenae's palm and thought back to the times between ad campaigns. Her parents were usually focused on their own careers, going to auditions or traveling to film on location. Cara seemed to disappear between takes.

"I seemed to fade out of their lives sometimes. I'd entertain myself by mimicking ads on television, practicing in case I had a chance at another part. Or I'd stay with my grandmother. She was a film actress, but she always seemed to find time to take me places. She never pushed me to act or pretended to take me on vacation when we were really going to an out-of-state audition."

Lenae squeezed Cara's hand. Her own mother had been tough on her—for good reason, since she didn't want Lenae growing up dependent or helpless—but there had never been any doubt of her love. Like Cara's family, though, affection had been doled out when Lenae accomplished something, not handed out freely when she wasn't earning it. "My mother was wonderful, but very achievement oriented. I understand what it's like to feel that love is a reward, not a given."

"It's lonely," Cara said, with little inflection in her voice. "Things got worse when I was older. At first, it was easy to get by as a cute baby or pretty little toddler, but eventually I needed more skill to back up my looks. I started losing out on parts as often as I booked them. My parents encouraged me to get into journalism, and they even tried to get me to study meteorology in college so I could do the weather on the news."

Lenae had to laugh at the thought of Cara spending her life predicting cold fronts and rainstorms. "I can't imagine you being satisfied with that kind of work," she said. "You seem too devoted to causes."

"I interview people who are devoted to causes, like you are."

Lenae shook her head, wishing she could erase the undeserved note of self-denigration she heard in Cara's voice. "You do more than that. And even though your parents pushed you into acting early, you seem energized by performing. It would exhaust me, but you really seem to enjoy it."

"I do. I hate to admit how much I love it, but it feels good to stand in front of a classroom or film one of my shows and know I'm reaching people with my words and expressions and gestures. I connect with the camera or with an audience, and it gives me a high I can't explain. Even early on, my brother Richard and I used to hang a sheet in the backyard and make up plays about animals and fairy sprites. Richard had been reading Shakespeare with Dad, so most of our plays were knockoffs of *A Midsummer Night's Dream* or *The Tempest*. We'd invite family and the neighbor kids, and it was a thrill to stand behind that old sheet and wait for my chance to go onstage." Cara paused and leaned her shoulder against Lenae's as if seeking comfort or reassurance. "I'm sure that sounds silly to you."

"Of course it doesn't." Lenae moved into the pressure from Cara's shoulder while the plane bumped and jostled them as it taxied to the runway. "I loved the excitement of working at the news station, the times when my words seemed to flow, and I knew the viewers would understand what I was trying to say. I sometimes felt excited or proud of what I wrote, but that didn't detract from the importance of the stories I told. I'd have loved to listen to one of your plays."

Cara frowned. The joy of those plays had been short-lived because once her parents recognized their interest and Richard's talent, even the simple games they played suddenly had structure and rules and fancy sets. Scripts from modern plays replaced the imaginative and silly ad-libbed ones. And while Richard had handled the post-performance critique sessions with a sense of humor and an ability not to take every criticism personally, Cara's love of performing had been tainted. Her brother had continued to move forward with his acting, not hesitating on the trajectory of a successful career. Cara's feelings of self-worth had been too tied to her parents' comments.

"The plays weren't anything special. I had fun, but I was never as good as Richard. Once my parents saw our interest in theater—amateur as it was—they stepped in and turned our games into training."

"But now you've found a way to be center stage while upholding your values. And because you're having fun on-camera, you're better able to express the optimism and hope in your stories."

Cara rested her head on Lenae's shoulder as the plane lifted into the air. Pickwick slid against her shins with a thud during the steep incline, but he didn't stop chewing on his bone. After Lenae's words, Cara felt more at peace than she had in ages. She had always felt slightly dirty enjoying the limelight, as if she was selling herself out for fame, but Lenae noticed more to her than that. Someone worthy doing something worthwhile. Was it wrong of her to enjoy the attention? Or was Lenae right in saying that Cara's enthusiasm for performing was a good and positive quality? Cara let the rumble of the engines and the steady chomp of dog teeth lull her toward sleep. She had always fought her attraction to performing. Maybe, just maybe, she could stop fighting and embrace that side of herself.

Chapter Eighteen

Cara paced around the hotel room. There wasn't much room for her to walk, especially since Pickwick insisted on being underfoot at all times.

She finally stopped and sat on the bed. Pickwick jumped up and sat next to her, and she put her arm around him and rubbed one of his favorite spots, between his shoulder blades. For all her fretting, the flight had been an easy one because Lenae had been there to help, to reassure, to laugh even when Pickwick destroyed the leather handle of her briefcase. Cara hadn't been much help to Lenae, but maybe that was for the best. Too many people had tried to help Lenae today, and she'd handled it with more poise than Cara would have been able to muster.

Lenae had said she understood the intentions behind the often pushy and sometimes downright rude assistance she received, but Cara believed Lenae was more bothered than she admitted. How could anyone be treated as less than human and not have it affect her somehow? Lenae was proud, fought to be seen as independent. She must hate being treated as a visually impaired person instead of simply as a person. Cara didn't have the same experiences, but she had been on the receiving end of comments and actions that diminished her—made her seem nothing more than a Bradley, nothing more than the surface of her skin.

Lenae's understanding words had helped, but Cara still struggled with her ambivalent feelings about tomorrow's morning show. She could have resisted more than she had or flatly refused to come, but she had been excited by the news. Torn. She didn't want to leave her job at the college or her public broadcasting show—places where she could perform while still believing she was doing something useful and not merely being vain. She didn't want to move her career into overdrive and face the cutthroat attitudes Lenae had dealt with at Three-N. But the idea of being interviewed on a national show and having a chance to prove she could hold her own with experienced media personalities thrilled her. She wasn't sure why and wasn't willing to think about what it might mean for her future if she enjoyed the spotlight more than she wanted.

Cara stood abruptly and Pickwick toppled on his side. She picked up his blue training cape and—as he always did when he realized they were going somewhere—he whirled in circles so she had a difficult time fastening him into his outfit.

Once he was ready, Cara knocked on the door connecting her room with Lenae's. She heard an indistinct invitation to enter and went into the other room. Pickwick pushed past her and jumped on Baxter where he sat next to Lenae. She was at the room's desk with a portable version of her office Brailler and piles of paperwork in front of her.

"Come on," Cara said. "We're going out."

"I really shouldn't. I brought the center's accounts with me and—"

"And you're going to put them back in your mangled briefcase and come out with me and Pickwick. Not because you want to, or because I want to, but because someday Pickwick's handler might want to go to a karaoke bar and unwind. What a travesty it'll be if Pickwick hasn't been exposed to one during his puppy-walking years."

Lenae laughed. She usually kept her life as orderly as possible. Objects, furniture, classes. All prearranged and set in the proper place. After an exhausting day of flying—and all the stress and indignities involved with the process—she would usually want nothing more than to fix the schematic of her hotel room in her mind and order room service. Then Baxter could be off duty and she could walk freely, without feeling every step. The idea of going out to dinner or a movie or, God forbid, a karaoke bar never would cross her mind. Why was she even considering it now? Pushing aside her monthly budget sheets and reaching for Baxter's harness? Because Cara needed to get out and get her mind off tomorrow's show. And because Lenae wanted to be the one to distract her.

They took the elevator downstairs, and she waited with the dogs while Cara checked with the hotel concierge and then led them onto the streets of New York.

"Where are we going?" Lenae asked. She dropped Baxter's harness and took Cara's arm as they walked. The near constant touch of Cara's arm or hand during the flight had stirred her senses. Every nerve ending seemed to tingle in Cara's presence, and she wanted to continue their contact. It felt more electric and alive than the energy of the city around them.

"A place called the Emerald Room. I asked for a bar that was low-key, but fun." Cara put her hand over Lenae's. "I can't believe you wanted to stay in tonight. We're in New York. How often can you say that?"

"I lived here for seven years," Lenae reminded her. She had loved the city for six of those years. Then, she'd wanted out as fast as possible and she'd found a new home where she didn't have to encounter constant reminders of her folly.

"Well, have you ever been to the Emerald Room?" Cara asked. She thought she heard a bitter note in Lenae's voice. She wondered what had happened during those seven years to make Lenae give up this city and her job as a newswriter. How had she ended up on a broken-down property in Washington?

"No. I must have missed that particular entertainment venue. I guess I spent too much of my time at the Met."

"You missed out. Or so I've heard from the concierge." Cara imagined Lenae dressed in satin, soaking up the notes of an opera.

Who had been sitting beside her? Someone as beautiful as Lenae, as dedicated and smart, wouldn't have been alone for long.

"I guess I did. Silly me, listening to some of the greatest voices on earth when I could have been hearing drunk versions of old Carpenters songs instead."

Cara pressed Lenae's hand against her side and felt the heat of her touch. Whoever had been part of Lenae's past, Cara was here now. Close beside her. "Exactly. Now if I'd been here with you, I'd have helped you broaden your horizons."

Lenae smiled in response, but her mind moved back in time. What if Cara had been here with her? An up-and-coming young reporter, spending time with one of the top writers? Would Cara have been any different from Traci, or would she, too, have used Lenae as a stepping stone on her career path? In a way, Cara had used her and her center as she moved from public broadcasting to the local news to a national morning show, but Lenae was having a difficult time attributing any mean-spirited intentions to Cara. Cara was fragmented, with her heart in one world and her inborn talent pushing her into another. She wanted to be behind the scenes, shifting the focus to the people working toward what she considered to be meaningful careers and charities. But at the same time, she loved the spotlight more than she wanted to. Traci had been single-mindedly moving upward. Cara kept pulling herself back.

Lenae's palm held Cara's firm upper arm, and the back of her hand rested against Cara's rib cage. "I believe my life in New York would have been more…interesting if you'd been here." She felt connected to every breath Cara took. If she'd known how Traci was going to use her, she'd never have taken the relationship to the bedroom. If she knew the same thing about Cara? She'd probably not be able to resist her anyway.

"Hmm. I'd like to know what word you were going to use in place of interesting," Cara said. "But I'll have to grill you about that later because we're here. It's time to sing."

"Time to listen to *you* sing," Lenae said as she walked through the door Cara held open. "If I did, both dogs would be howling."

"We'll do a quartet," Cara said. She guided Lenae to a table against the wall and placed her hand on the back of a chair. "I'll get us a couple of drinks and make sure the management is okay with our dogs being here. Will you be able to control both Pickwick and Baxter?"

"Of course." Lenae sat down and shifted her feet to make room for Baxter. She pointed under the table. "Under here, Pickwick. Lie down with Baxter. I'll have a whiskey and Coke, please."

Cara watched in disbelief as her puppy curled in a ball next to the empty chair. He stared at Lenae with his tongue hanging out and a look of adoration on his face. "Incredible. I'll buy you a double if you can teach me how to do that."

"Trade secret," Lenae said. "Or I just happened to give him the command when he was tired and wanted to lie down."

"That I can believe." Cara went to the bar and ordered a cosmo and Lenae's drink. She looked back at the table while she waited and watched Lenae sway gently and sensually to the music. Cara licked her lips and turned her attention to her surroundings. There were fewer than twenty people in the room, most appearing settled in like regulars—Cara wondered if they were permanently attached to their barstools or if they eventually went home. The stage was empty, but she could see the words to a Michael Jackson song scrolling across the screen, apparently in case someone found the energy to get up and sing. The concierge had gotten low-key right, but the fun aspect was debatable.

"Here you go." The bartender handed her a tray with their drinks as well as a couple of plastic cups and two bottles of water. "And some water for your dogs. Here, take them some peanuts, too."

"Thanks," Cara said, putting the cost of the drinks and a generous tip on the bar. She balanced the tray in her hands and slowly made her way back to the table.

"Is the room really emerald colored?" Lenae asked after she took a sip of her drink.

Cara looked around. The décor was anything but classy, and Lenae looked as out of place as a princess in a dive bar. "Yes, sort of. The walls are covered in a green-velvet embossed paper—I think it's called flocking. The carpet is the color of pine trees, where it isn't threadbare. The chairs and lampshades are a lighter color—more grass-like—and the lamps have fringe on them. It's all very 1970s."

"Are we in a bar, or a brothel?"

"Too early to tell." Cara offered the dogs a cup of water before taking a drink of her cosmo. "No one seems to have enough energy to sing, let alone have sex."

"Why don't you get them started?" Lenae bit her lip and smiled. "I meant singing, of course."

"You're blushing," Cara said. She rarely saw Lenae off balance in any way and knew Lenae would probably welcome a change in subject, but she decided to take advantage of the small slip in her composure and press her for information. "I'll sing later. For now, tell me why you left Three-N. You have a natural gift and belong in the dog-training profession, but why'd you make such a drastic change?"

Lenae reached down and rubbed Baxter's ear. He turned his head and licked her hand before dropping his nose on his paws again. "I guess in some ways I lost my confidence, and in others I found the confidence I needed to pursue my calling. Not that training dogs was something I'd wanted to do all my life. I'd never considered a career helping other visually impaired people, even after I got Baxter and fell in love with him and with the freedom he gave me. My mom raised me herself, and she insisted I be part of the sighted world. No excuses or allowances. We never had pets at home, and Baxter was my first."

Cara kept silent while Lenae talked, even though the story was being told in fragments. She'd piece it together later, but she didn't want to interrupt now.

"I loved writing and got into journalism when I was in high school. I wrote for the school paper and it seemed a natural career move for me. I liked the fast pace of newswriting, the constant change and challenge. I still think I'm better suited for the work I used to do. I dealt with facts and details and deadlines, and let the anchors and reporters do the work of conveying emotions and intent to the audience. Connecting with people hasn't been a strong suit of mine—well, you saw what it was like today, with everyone trying to help me. It doesn't take long before you start to avoid any sort of contact, or before you're suspicious of any offer of help because it makes you look weak."

Cara watched Lenae's finger trace the rim of her glass. She seemed to be circling around the reason she left her job, but like spokes on a wheel, every aspect was connected. Her doubts about Gene and Toby, her desire to be independent, all of it…all rotating around a focal point she hadn't yet mentioned.

"I didn't date much after I got the job with Three-N. The stress was always high, but after a few years I adjusted to it. I got Baxter, and my life outside work suddenly was so much easier. I had freedom and time I hadn't ever had before. So when Traci asked me out—she was a new correspondent and everyone agreed she was going to go far in the business—I said yes. I always believed I had some sort of secret ability to read people, as if my other senses were stronger because I wasn't fooled by appearances or expressions. But I couldn't read Traci. Or maybe I could at first, but when she saw an opportunity…"

Pickwick sat up and rested his chin on Cara's thigh. She fed him a couple of peanuts. "What'd she do to you?"

Lenae swallowed a third of her drink in one gulp. "I did it to myself. There was a new feature show in the works, one that I knew would be perfect for her. She was being courted by other networks at the time, so I told her about the opportunity even though we hadn't officially announced it yet. I wanted to keep her there with me. I trusted her to be discreet…well, I simply trusted her. I asked her to wait for the chance instead of leaving Three-N."

Lenae paused and Cara fed Pickwick some more peanuts. He was staying surprisingly quiet, and she didn't want him to break Lenae's train of thought before she finished her story.

"I hear Pickwick chewing. What are you feeding him?"

"Just peanuts. Go on. Did she tell someone higher in the network that you'd told her? Were you fired?"

"No. She took the idea and pitched it to CNN. They bought it and hired her. We had to scrap the concept, of course, but I wasn't fired. No one seemed surprised by what had happened, as if they assumed that type of subterfuge and betrayal was just an acceptable part of the business."

Cara thought of her own family. Would her mom steal a story concept from her network and pitch it to another if she thought a raise or a better part would be in her future? Would her dad do the same? Sadly, she didn't have any trouble imagining either one taking advantage of what they'd see as a golden opportunity. They had been excited when she'd had the chance to use Lenae's center and the puppy-walking program to promote herself. No wonder Lenae had been skeptical about giving her Pickwick—how much worse a betrayal if she were to use not only Lenae but also the animals for her own advantage.

"So you left on principle." Would she be strong enough to do the same thing?

"Yes. I couldn't believe she'd used me like that. Well, after the fact I could identify warning signs I'd missed along the way. I guess my real shock was due to my inability to really know who she was. I thought I saw the person underneath the surface, but I was as much a fool as anyone. Through all of it, Baxter was constant and loyal. No agenda beyond caring for me. I didn't want to work in a business where Traci's behavior wasn't just tolerated but was accepted as the norm. And I wanted to give other people a chance to find the same connection and trust I'd found with Baxter. Unfortunately, the human equation is tripping me up again. I can train the dogs, but I can't read the people well enough to reach them."

"You've taught me a lot already, and I never had a pet before getting Pickwick. You're teaching me how to communicate with him, but I don't have the natural sense of how to do it, like you do. Does that mean you're a failure, or does it just mean I'm learning at my own pace and in my own way?"

Lenae thought about Cara's words. She believed Cara was learning faster and better than she gave herself credit for, even though she still didn't have Lenae's quiet confidence with Pickwick. She'd get there, but it was a process. Lenae didn't have Cara's natural talent for communicating with people, but maybe she'd get where she needed to be in her own time.

"You know what you need?" Cara asked. Lenae heard her take a drink, and then the clunk of an empty-sounding glass landing on the table. "You need to belt out your frustration in a song."

"You seem determined to get me up there, but I've listened to your voice enough to assume you're a great singer. I'll sound like a donkey braying in comparison."

"Want to know a secret?" Cara asked, leaning close to Lenae's ear. Lenae felt a shiver run down her spine at the feel of Cara's breath against her skin.

"What?" she asked, her own voice sounding breathless.

"I'm tone deaf."

Lenae laughed, relieved to have some release from the tension caused by Cara's nearness. "Right. I believe that."

"You will after the first song. I can't carry a tune despite ten years of expensive music lessons. Remember, I was in training to be a stage actress from early on, so I had tap and jazz and singing classes almost daily. I was a glorious failure at all of them—enjoying every moment, but unable to master any of the skills."

Cara stood and grabbed Lenae's hand, trying to pull her to her feet.

Lenae resisted her still. "I hate to break it to you, but the concierge misled you when she recommended this as a fun karaoke bar. We've been here almost an hour and no one has sung anything."

"So, we'll start. Come on Baxter, Pickwick." Lenae felt both dogs jump to their feet, obviously ready to follow Cara onstage. "Hey, they're paying attention to me. Good boy, Pickwick."

Baxter licked Lenae's hand and she took hold of his harness and stood up. "I seem to be outnumbered. Okay, one song."

She listened as Cara paged through the song list. She wanted to leave, to protest that she wouldn't be able to read the prompter on the karaoke machine, but Cara had apparently been sensitive to Lenae's situation. She led Lenae onstage and handed her one of the microphones, giving her the dimensions of the stage in a quiet voice as the intro to "Everlasting Love" started.

"Baxter, find the door," Lenae said, but Cara heard the humor in her voice, a playful easiness that hadn't been there while she'd talked about Traci and Three-N.

"Ignore that command, Baxter," Cara said. Baxter didn't seem inclined to lead Lenae off the stage, anyway. Lenae heard him and Pickwick wrestling in the excitement of doing something new. The puppy seemed to be feeding off Cara's almost frantic good mood, and Lenae felt herself responding to it as well. What a pair she and Cara made. She didn't trust herself anymore to see beyond anyone's surface image, and Cara wasn't sure if she had anything below her own surface appearance even if someone took the time to look. But for tonight, they could be allies against a world that seemed to value appearances above all else.

The lyrics must have begun flashing by on the screen because Cara started to sing, shaking Lenae from her philosophical musing. Lenae winced dramatically at Cara's first notes, but she joined in as soon as Cara reached the chorus, quietly at first, but gaining volume as the audience started to clap along with the music.

Lenae moved to the music and tried to match Cara's intensity with her singing. She at least could hear when she and Cara were off-key, but she wasn't a good enough singer to do anything about it. Surprisingly, Cara had been exactly right about this being the cure for Lenae's gloomy mood after her confession.

She had spent her life trying to be perfect at independence, her jobs, at managing her life. How fun to do something with gusto, knowing full well she was going to suck at it, and reveling in the imperfect result. She looped one arm through Cara's and felt Baxter's happy panting against her other hand as she sang, feeling her world condense to this stage, this meaningful connection with Cara and Baxter, even as she shouted out the words to the corny song.

CHAPTER NINETEEN

Lenae was silent as they walked back to the hotel. Baxter moved quickly along the sidewalk, seemingly eager to get back to the hotel for some good sleep after a long and busy day. Pickwick was asleep in Cara's arms. Lenae had spent plenty of evenings relaxing, but she couldn't remember the last time she had gone out and had so much fun. Song after song, until her throat was sore from the exertion and her facial muscles felt stretched and tired from smiling so much.

"I hadn't realized how much Pickwick has grown," Cara said when they got in the elevator. She leaned against Lenae's shoulder on the ride up to the fourteenth floor. "He's turning into a dog. Size-wise, at least. He's still a puppy in the brains department."

"He had a lot of new experiences today," Lenae said. She reached over and rubbed his head, letting the back of her hand brush against Cara's chin as she pulled it back. "You've been a great puppy walker. He has a natural curiosity and a good attitude, but the way he accepts all the changes and different environments is a testament to you and how you've raised him."

"Thank you," Cara said quietly. "I was a little antagonistic when I talked to you about the puppy walkers the first day we met, but I've learned a lot about the job since then. I'll be sad to say good-bye to him, but every step of the way I'm thinking ahead and figuring out what he needs now in order to be a good partner in the future."

"A *little* antagonistic? As I recall, I used the word belligerent when I told Des about our conversation." She put her arm around Cara's shoulders to let her know she was teasing. "But I've been impressed by the way you've taken responsibility for him. You're shaping the dog he'll become. It's an enormous undertaking, to work so hard so someone you've never met will benefit from the training you've done. And Pickwick will be better able to bond with his person and enjoy his work because of you."

Cara turned her head and kissed Lenae's temple. "Thank you."

Lenae let go of Cara as they walked off the elevator and down the hall. She had been drawn to Cara from the start, feeling a physical attraction even when she thought they were too different to ever connect on a more emotional, personal level. Tonight had been full of playful touching and laughter, but as they got closer to their rooms, she felt a stillness settle over them. She wanted Cara—had wanted her from the start—but when they were onstage singing together, she had imagined them rushing back to the hotel and falling through the door in a tangled heap onto the bed. But the quietness between them unsettled her. She had thought Cara might want her, too, but maybe she was wrong.

"We're here," Cara said. She supported Pickwick with one arm while she got her key card out of her back pocket and inserted it into her door's lock. She saw Lenae about to do the same thing, but she took the card out of Lenae's hand. "Why don't you come visit with me for a while? I can open the doors between our rooms so Baxter can have his bed."

Lenae followed her into the room and took off Baxter's harness and lead. He shook himself before trotting into Lenae's room and jumping on the bed. He turned in a circle and settled down, so Cara carried Pickwick over and laid him next to Baxter. When she got back to her room, Lenae was sitting on the edge of her bed, her expression as uncertain as Cara felt.

Cara sat beside her and framed Lenae's face with her hands. She closed her eyes and brushed her thumbs across Lenae's cheekbones, using her fingertips to trace the shape of her cheeks and eyebrows and forehead, as if for the first time. As if she hadn't already memorized the contours of Lenae's face with her eyes. The curve of Lenae's lips was imprinted in her mind, but she slowly outlined them with her index finger as if to map the territory before she leaned forward and pressed her own lips against Lenae's.

A mutual intake of breath, a smile of recognition. Cara felt Lenae's responses as they mirrored her own in the gentle, almost chaste, kiss.

"I expected a tidal wave." Cara pulled back but kept her eyes closed.

"Disappointed?" Lenae asked.

"No way," Cara said. She struggled to explain the way the room had seemed to tilt, even though they were sitting so still. "I've wanted to kiss you for a long time, but I expected it to be kind of wild. Like the surface of the ocean during a storm. Not…"

"Not a deep, strong current." Lenae finished her sentence.

"Exactly." Cara moved forward into another kiss, this one more forceful than the last. She'd felt passion before, but nothing like this. She was floating, then sinking, barely able to catch her breath.

Lenae parted her lips and felt Cara's tongue slide between them. For once, she was acting without worrying about direction. She had no goals for this relationship, no five-year plan. Just tonight. She pushed Cara back on the bed and leaned over her.

"Don't move," she said, leaving a trail of kisses along Cara's jaw. "You've been able to see me, but I haven't learned you yet. Let me touch you."

She put her hand flat on Cara's chest. *Start with the heart of her. Not her hair, her chin, her face. But her heart, where she truly needs to be known.* Lenae cupped Cara's breast and felt her heartbeat, strong and fast. She moved her hand, wanting the friction of Cara's silky shirt against skin to increase Cara's arousal. She followed the edge of Cara's shirt with her fingers, from her shoulder to the V between her breasts and back again until she felt Cara arch up toward her hand. She dropped her head and used her lips to follow the same path.

Cara arched her back even deeper, needing to be closer to Lenae. She had been touched, had felt her body respond to other women, but she had kept her form and her distinction before. Lenae unbuttoned her shirt and her hands kneaded Cara's breasts, and Cara felt shapeless. Lenae was molding her into something new and more alive.

She heard her own gasp as Lenae circled her nipple with an almost-not-there touch, only to switch to a demanding pull with her lips. Cara pressed forward, eager to get as much of herself as she could into the warm wetness of Lenae's mouth. She wouldn't look, refused to open her eyes, wanting to feel what Lenae felt.

She reached for Lenae's hips when she shifted away, but Lenae stayed just out of reach. Her fingers sifted through Cara's hair, and Cara felt the touch from her scalp to the tips of each strand. Light pressure along her eyebrows and the bones of her face. Every indentation and curve examined and made new by Lenae's touch. Neck, arms, waist. Cara wriggled under Lenae's thorough exploration of her body, unable to remain still and barely able to restrain her impulse to touch back. She wanted Lenae to know her, but the intensity of Lenae's focus was almost too much to bear. She felt as if Lenae's fingers dipped beneath her skin when they circled and probed her navel, along the top of her thigh, between her eagerly spreading legs. She felt a moment of fear that Lenae wouldn't like what she found under Cara's quivering surface—or, worse, that she wouldn't find anything beyond the soft skin and well-proportioned bone structure—but she drew confidence from Lenae's sharp groan when her fingers slipped through Cara's wetness.

The sound from Lenae, at once pleased and almost painful, was Cara's cue to move. To anchor her fingers in Lenae's hair and pull her forward for a drowning kiss. First a clashing of teeth and tongues, but softening to a barely perceptible brush of lips before exploding with force again. Waves of movement, thrusting forward and receding, over and over until Cara had to pull away, to cry out as her orgasm crashed over and through her.

Cara curled toward Lenae. Usually she'd be almost anxious to turn to her partner in bed, to get the attention off herself and onto someone else. But she basked in Lenae's arms and let Lenae softly stroke her until the ripples of her climax eased.

Lenae marveled at the way Cara's body had responded to her touch—the way it responded even now, in its sated state. She felt the same release, as if she had come when Cara did, but her body awakened again when Cara burrowed her face in Lenae's neck and bit gently along the tendon from her ear to her collarbone.

She rolled on her back in response to pressure from Cara's hands, feeling Cara's leg nudge between her own. Cara's hands moved from her waist to her back, forcing Lenae to arch and make room for them as they slid along her spine and then curled forward to grip her shoulders. She wrapped her legs around Cara and pulled her flush against her body, limbs intertwined until Lenae had no way of telling where her own body left off and Cara's began. She twisted her head and kissed Cara's fingers where they clenched her at the base of her neck.

They moved as one organism, the energy of Lenae's growing arousal seeming to fuel Cara's hips as they pressed Lenae more and more firmly into the mattress. With each grinding motion, Lenae felt an answering gush of liquid and the film of sweat breaking out on her body—or was it Cara's? Or both? The friction between her thighs and the slippery joining of the rest of their skin brought Lenae to climax, all too soon. She felt her own shuddering release echo through Cara as the intensity of their connection coalesced into a soft, steady kiss from Cara's lips against her own.

CHAPTER TWENTY

Lenae woke up with the feeling she was caught in a vise. She took a few moments to reorient herself, patting the bedcovers to figure out how she'd gotten trapped. Pickwick was draped over her legs, pinning her in place. The familiar bulk of Baxter stretched against her back, blocking any movement in that direction. Unfamiliar, but very welcome and enticing, was the Creamsicle scent of Cara, who was spooned in Lenae's arms.

"Mmm. I can move my legs in bed for the first time in weeks," Cara mumbled in a sleep-thick voice. "It feels wonderful."

"I'm sure it does." Lenae laughed and nibbled on Cara's ear. "Unfortunately, I can't move mine."

"That's your fault for being the dog whisperer." Cara sighed and burrowed closer to Lenae. "Let's just skip the filming and stay in bed all day."

At the mention of the morning show, Lenae felt her body stiffen. Baxter raised his head and gave a small whine before resting his chin on her ribcage. "We should get these two fed and out for a walk," Lenae said. "You need to be at the studio in just over an hour."

"*We* need to be at the studio," Cara corrected her, but Lenae had already gotten out of bed and was feeling along the wall for the adjoining door.

"I'll take a quick shower and we'll meet you and Pickwick in the hall." Lenae went into her room and shut the door between them.

She leaned against the door for a moment, relieved to have some space to think, but already missing the feel of Cara's soft warmth. At the sound of Baxter's quiet whine, she walked easily through the room—unhindered by anyone else's belongings—and got his breakfast ready. She got in a scalding-hot shower while he ate, hoping in vain that the heat would sear Cara's touch from her skin. The night had been wonderful, and something Lenae had wanted for a long time. Beautiful sex, laughter, fun. But how much of the night would end this morning? How much of the union had been Cara's way of working off nervous energy before her big show today? Lenae braced her hands against the wall of the shower and replayed Cara's orgasm in her mind. Whatever the day brought, whatever their future together, she now had a mass of sensations and smells and movements that would always be connected with her thoughts of Cara.

Lenae leaned back in her chair and mustered all her willpower to keep from swatting away the mascara wand and running out the door. She'd had to put up with the hair-and-makeup crew for the weekly spot with Cara and Pickwick, but they had been fairly unobtrusive and quick. Today she felt like she was being made up by students from the local clown college. Her face felt heavy and unnatural, and she was getting more and more uneasy as the morning progressed.

Cara, meanwhile, seemed in her element. She chatted and joked with the stylists, discussing hairdos and wardrobe choices as if her very life depended on the image she portrayed on television. If Lenae hadn't spent so much time with Cara, both on- and off-camera, she might have believed Cara's heart and soul were tied to this morning's show, but she knew her well enough to hear the subtle changes in her voice and inflection. Cara was already in on-camera mode. She had become someone different the moment she walked onto the set. Was this her real self or her way of coping with the appearance-oriented world? Was she retreating deeper within herself the more she projected her bubblier personality outward?

Lenae still hadn't had a chance to process the events of last night. Events. She shook her head at her detached way of describing the consuming sex she and Cara had shared, but her stylist gripped her chin to hold her still, applying mascara without pause. Lenae hadn't wanted to think about last night, to wonder where it left them and where they went from here, because she was too nervous about this show. Parading around with Baxter, possibly making a fool of herself. She was out of her element and not happy about it. So she had escaped from Cara's room this morning, closing the door between them like a coward.

When she had met Cara for their walk, Cara had been too cranky to be able to talk about anything except for the expensive jeans Pickwick had shredded while Cara was in the shower. So they had spent the cab ride to the studio in strained silence, with no touch between them except for the occasional and accidental brush of hands when they both reached for the door handle at the same time. From full-body, mind-to-mind contact to an unbridgeable gulf was too much for Lenae to handle with gracefulness. She felt adrift.

Lenae felt herself mentally slipping further from the action going on around her. She'd discovered a rare, and unsettling, gift in junior high—the ability to distance herself from the conversations and actions taking place right around her. Not only did she feel separate, but she seemed to waft out of the minds of those around her as well. She had been able to hear conversations about herself and others as if everyone had forgotten she was in the room. It was the trigger for her realization that some people believed that if she couldn't see, she couldn't hear or even understand either. As an adult, the dehumanizing effect was disturbing, but the skill came in handy at times, when she wanted to escape the world and be left alone with Baxter.

She sat very still, her hand resting on Baxter to remind herself of his unwavering companionship, and listened to the disjointed talk around her. She'd pick up threads of conversations, or follow one voice—usually Cara's—for several sentences before moving to another. She wasn't trying to eavesdrop, just to feel as if she were an aural observer instead of a participant in this crazy day.

Most of the talk centered around Cara. The people nearest her, most likely drawn to her beauty and inclusive way of speaking, were engaged with her. But Cara was also the subject of conversation for those farther away from her. Lenae only needed a few moments as a fly on the wall to learn that a position of host for the morning show would be opening up soon, and the studio grapevine had Cara pegged as favorite for the role.

❖

Cara kept up her incessant chatter with the stylists and producers who drifted by her makeup station. She was irritable and confused about her night with Lenae, and the more she felt like escaping the studio, the more bright and entertaining she tried to appear. She had to hide her feelings and get through the day somehow. Make a strong pitch for Lenae's center and show Pickwick off as the charmer he was—even though she was going to miss her best pair of jeans. Oh, and maybe, just maybe, get her parents off her case. Do the show to appease them and be done with it.

But the more time she spent at the studio, the more uneasy she felt. Half-finished sentences and thinly veiled hints made her aware of something going on below the surface of today's show. Something more permanent than a quick promo for herself and the center. Cara looked for Lenae, needing someone to talk to, but Lenae had disappeared. She was still sitting in her chair of course, close by Cara's, but the look in her eyes was distant and untouchable. Worse than Lenae's shuttered expression was the way people began to move around her as if she wasn't there. As if they were moving *through* her. And Lenae seemed to be encouraging the illusion.

"I see you," Cara said, raising her voice slightly. Lenae turned her head in Cara's direction. "Yes, you. Stop trying to hide."

She caught Lenae's quick smile before it was hidden again. But when they walked on to the set to do their demonstrations, Lenae bumped into Cara's side and gave her hand a brief squeeze. The connection, minimal as it was, gave Cara the strength to get through the show with the right amount of animation. Not too falsely bright and cheery, but not nervous and hesitant. Her improving mood seemed to feed Lenae's as well, and the banter between them as they discussed Pickwick's wild ways made the audience laugh.

Cara enjoyed the format of the show, with its cameras and live audience, sort of a combination of her television show and teaching a class at Evergreen. She felt at ease answering questions about the puppy-walking experience and helping Lenae as she demonstrated Baxter's guiding abilities. She had done enough on-air work to know when a segment was going to be popular and accessible, and theirs was. She should have felt a high after finishing, but she didn't. She was proud of herself for holding her own on a meticulously produced national show. She was thrilled with Lenae's performance and with the way Baxter and Pickwick had followed their lead and hammed it up for the audience. But she felt something missing at the end of the segment.

"Great job, you two," the host said when they finished and her stylist had come over to do some touch-ups before the next spot. Cara sat with her hand casually resting on the back of Lenae's chair while Baxter trotted around to various audience members with his harness in his mouth. "Feel free to get some breakfast backstage, and Marty will find you seats if you want to stay and watch the rest of the show."

"Oh, okay. Thank you," Cara said. Lenae got to her feet and called Baxter over to her, but Cara hesitated. "I was hoping to talk to you about some of your past guests. Like the author Ron Campton. It must have been a thrill to meet him."

"I wasn't doing his interview, so I didn't talk to him. Sorry."

Even though her voice was friendly, Cara didn't miss the note of dismissal. She wanted to stay, to chat with the audience like she did after the formal filming of her own show, when everyone let down their guard and became real. Or even like she'd talked to Lenae on their first day of filming, when they had disagreed because each felt passionately about the subject of puppy walking. She had learned something that day and now had Pickwick in her life. She had loved talking to the Baers after the cameras shut off and she had a chance to get to know each small child.

Funny. She hadn't slipped back into her old cynical ways since the day she'd met Lenae. Maybe because she had been at the center after the show was filmed and she had seen that Lenae didn't just put on a show of caring and devoting her life to a cause. She lived it, every moment. Cara had filmed a couple of episodes of *Around the Sound* since then and had actually allowed herself to believe that the kindness, the altruism people showed on film wasn't just for the cameras, didn't disappear once she and the crew were gone.

But this morning's taping had been an eye-opener, reminding her how this industry operated, how the camera lied. The host had been all smiles and gushing praise of Baxter and Pickwick, but once the spot was in the can, she was ready to move on to something new, with equal enthusiasm. In this case, a pop star who was designing swimsuits for a department store chain. She couldn't really blame the host who was, after all, just doing her job. Performing.

Lenae finished buckling Baxter's harness and stood. When she reached out, Cara grabbed her hand, holding on to it as if it were the only real thing in the studio.

"Do you want to get some food? Or find a seat in the audience?" Lenae asked.

Cara wrapped Pickwick's leash around one wrist and tucked her other hand in Lenae's elbow. "What I want is to meander back to our hotel and order room service."

CHAPTER TWENTY-ONE

W here do you want to go?" Lenae asked once they were back outside on the crowded sidewalk. She felt Cara close beside her and couldn't resist touching her arm, for companionship and not comfort. She had been intimidated by the New York crowds for the first month or two when she had moved to the city, but she had quickly grown accustomed to the energy of so many people milling past her.

"I want to feel *your* New York," Cara said, leaning close to Lenae's ear when she spoke.

Distracted by the rush of soft breath, Lenae hesitated for a moment. "You mean my old apartment? The Three-N building?" She'd take Cara to those places if she wanted, but retracing the steps she had taken with Traci would be painful for her.

"Not so literal. I don't know how to explain, but when we walked down to the Sound when you came to Evergreen, you seemed to experience it more deeply than I did. Every sense attuned to your surroundings. I *see* places, but not as dimensionally as you *know* them."

"Not all the time," Lenae said. She paused while she listened to the noises around her. She didn't usually dwell on how much she actually perceived, or that she experienced things differently than a sighted person. "Sometimes I walk without noticing the world around me and sometimes I scarf down a cheeseburger without tasting it. But I do have to be aware of more than a single sense."

"So show me your New York."

"You'll have to close your eyes."

"And let Pickwick guide me?"

"No way," Lenae said with a laugh. "He'll march you right in front of a speeding cab. Just close your eyes and tell me what you smell."

Cara gripped Lenae's arm and stood silently for a moment. "Breathe normally," Lenae told her. "You don't need to sniff like Pickwick around a tree trunk."

Cara punched her lightly on the arm. "Fine. Breathe normally. All I smell is exhaust. No, there's more. Chanel. It's yours, but it's on *my* skin after last night."

"Mmm. Good start," Lenae said. The memory of having Cara in full-body contact with her made her ache deep inside. "Why don't we continue this exercise in my hotel room?"

"That's where I plan to end it," Cara said. "Wait, I'm getting something else. Yeast, I think, or fresh bread. Greasy meat. Are you hungry?"

"That's why I suggested the hotel room," Lenae said, but she caught the same smells Cara had detected and her stomach growled.

"My newly acute hearing tells me you want lunch," Cara said.

"I do. Keep your eyes closed, and we'll have Baxter find the restaurant. If there's greasy meat involved, he'll take us there with no problem."

They moved along the sidewalk a bit awkwardly as Baxter led Lenae, with Cara clutching her arm, and Pickwick trying to go in his own direction. Lenae had expected the morning of filming to turn into an all-day event as Cara networked at the studio, so she was thrilled to have a private day with her instead. She had been prepared to let last night be a fling, but her foolish heart was ready to extend the intimacy as long as possible.

Lenae opened the door for her bulky entourage. "Can you tell the type of food we'll be eating?" she asked Cara, curious about how many clues she'd catch.

"I still smell hamburger and grease. Something fried. McDonald's?"

Lenae laughed. "I think this place serves Russian food. I smell boiled potatoes and dill. Plus, the people at the table near us are speaking Russian."

"Cheater," Cara said. "You only told me to use my nose."

"Next we'll experience the world of taste," Lenae said once they were seated, with the dogs settled under the table. "Open your eyes and go into the bathroom while I order our food, so you don't know what we're having."

She heard the scrape of Cara's chair and her footsteps as she walked away, but Cara came back almost immediately.

"Are you sure that's a good idea? How do I know what you'll be sticking in my mouth?" Cara teased.

"You didn't have any complaints last night," Lenae said. She smiled when Cara made a sound between a cough and a groan. "Don't you trust me?"

"Completely."

Lenae ordered a variety of dishes while she thought about Cara's admission. Once the waitress had left, she asked herself the same question. Did she trust Cara? When they'd first met, she would have answered with an emphatic no, but everything had changed. Or rather, nothing had changed. Cara was still the same person she had been, but now Lenae knew her. And trusted her, with her heart and soul.

Although her thoughts were serious, Lenae was able to laugh and enjoy her lunch with Cara. She fed her bites of food—luckily Pickwick was on hand to clean the floor of any dropped pieces—and let Cara try to guess the ingredients of each one. Their lighthearted companionship, something Lenae hadn't expected to last beyond the karaoke bar, seemed to be the new norm for them. Touch was no longer an accidental or infrequent thing, as it had been in the past. Now they connected frequently and with a possessiveness Lenae was surprised to find she enjoyed.

"Do you know what you just ate?" she asked, wiping her thumb across Cara's mouth in case she had dropped any flakes of pastry.

"Something with spinach, yuk. And dough."

"A knish," Lenae said. She fed a piece of the potato dumpling to each of the dogs. "Are you getting full? We can go outside and try sense number three."

"Are we at touch yet?"

"We haven't stopped touching all day," Lenae said. She wanted to be back in the room with Cara, alone with her and naked, but she was reluctant at the same time. Would this last between them once the trip was over? Was it a city-specific fling, or something real? Lenae didn't know how to ask.

Cara kept her eyes pressed closed while Lenae paid their bill and walked her back to the sidewalk. She felt the touch of the sun on her face, but it didn't compare with the heat where Lenae was holding her arm. Unexpected and wonderful. Last night, the easy banter during the show, this experience with senses. Cara hadn't had time to think about where they were going. She was just enjoying the feeling of traveling together for the moment.

"Now, listen," Lenae said.

Cara felt her close, got lost in the breathy timbre of Lenae's voice. She didn't care if she heard anything else.

"What do you hear?"

"Cars driving by. Honking horns. People talking."

"Okay, that's what you expect to hear. Now think about sound as a vibration. What do you *feel*?"

Cara grew still. Lenae was right. Cara hadn't really been hearing the traffic and the people around her. She knew they were there, so she named them. She tuned into her own heartbeat, then to the charge between her and Lenae, as real as if it were an electrical current connecting them. She heard the dogs moving on the pavement. Other footsteps. As her awareness spread out, she noticed a bird far away, the clop of a horse's hooves, and the smoother sound of the cart it pulled. She felt the music of the city seep inside her.

"Is that the subway?" she asked, opening her eyes in surprise.

"Yes, I felt it, too. Rumbling away underground. Amazing what you can hear when you let yourself feel."

"Speaking of touch," Cara said. She had enjoyed the lesson in environmental immersion, but she was hungry for more than lunch now. "Why don't we go back to the hotel and I'll take over for the last two senses?"

"Sounds good to me," Lenae said.

Cara hailed a cab even though they were easily within walking distance of the hotel. She had waited long enough, with Lenae holding her arm and feeding her bites of food. The sensations had piled up until Cara thought she might burst with awareness if she didn't have Lenae to herself.

She took over for Baxter and led them into the elevator and down the hall to her room. "Do you want to know what I see and feel?" Cara asked.

"Yes," Lenae whispered. She linked her arms around Cara's neck.

"I see lips slightly open, waiting to be kissed. They're beautiful and pink, but I remember how red and bruised by kisses they were this morning. And I see just the tip of your very talented tongue. I remember *that* from last night, too."

Lenae laughed and Cara swooped in for a kiss while her mouth was relaxed and open. Lenae's tongue, merely hinted at before, slid over her own. Cara sucked it deeply into her mouth before letting it go. "The textures of you amaze me," she said, punctuating her words with soft touches from her fingertips. "Your tongue is rough. And your teeth"—Cara laughed as Lenae bit her finger—"are sharp. Your lips are soft, but it's a different kind of soft than the skin of your cheek or your inner thigh. I love the tingle on my skin when I brush my hand through your hair or over the downy curl of your lashes."

Cara pulled Lenae's shirt over her head and unhooked her bra. She cupped Lenae's small breasts and rubbed her thumbs over her nipples. "I love how tight and hard you get when I touch you. Goose bumps, like you're getting a chill, but your skin is fiery hot. When I see you arch your back and push your breasts toward me, I almost lose my mind."

Cara leaned over and took a taut nipple into her mouth. She sucked gently, gliding her tongue over the puckered surface of Lenae's tender skin. She pulled her head back and laughed as Lenae tightened her hold on the back of Cara's head and urged her forward. "Your grip changes," she said. "You hold me tight sometimes, tugging on my hair. And gently other times, like a caress. And when you orgasm? Your hand goes limp but stays tangled, close to my scalp."

"What else...do you feel?" Lenae asked with a gasp as Cara knelt in front of her and pushed her back against the closed door.

Cara unbuttoned Lenae's slacks and slid them and her underwear to the floor. She put her hands against Lenae's thighs and pressed her legs apart. "I feel muscles, strong from so much walking. Tendons that contract when you're trying to pull me deeper inside you. A wetness that's more welcoming and healing than the finest spa on earth."

Lenae's fingers clenched in Cara's hair. "Tell me...more."

Cara made lazy circles with her fingers around Lenae's wet lips. "You're full of fascinating textures here, too. Some places are smooth, others rough. Soft and hard at the same time. Your muscles clench like you're powerful, but weak enough to collapse. Your skin moves under my fingers when you start to shiver and your inner thigh muscles tremble. And when you come?" Cara asked as Lenae's orgasm crashed over her. "When you come, I feel and taste and smell and hear and see...heaven."

Chapter Twenty-two

Lenae stood in her closet and sifted through her outfits. She had everything carefully arranged by color, by seasonal fabric, and by function. She had work clothes from her old job and casual outfits suitable for training dogs. She didn't have any date-with-Cara clothes.

She chose navy slacks and a silver silk shirt from her business clothes. The premiere of a new play at Seattle's ACT would be dressy, but not formal. She had been surprised when Cara called and invited her to the opening night. She had spoken to Cara's dad, of course, but had never met any of her family. She wasn't expecting warmth and cuddliness from them, not after some of the stories Cara had told her, but she knew the level of talent she could expect from them. She had read reviews of the play and was looking forward to hearing Cara's brother in the starring role, but even more, she was curious about what it would be like to be out with Cara. Their karaoke night had been a sort of date, but this was different. Meeting the girlfriend's parents in a way, although those words hadn't been explicitly spoken. She'd be in Cara's hometown, in her milieu, around her family. Lenae had no doubt Cara would be affected by all the variables, and she wasn't sure what to expect. The on-air Cara, or the woman who had become her lover?

Lenae groomed Baxter before brushing her own hair and getting dressed. She had spent two days in New York with Cara last week, not being apart from her for more than a few minutes at a time. Wonderful days, but separate from daily life. Lenae came back to her settled life here at the center, but Cara's future was less certain. She hadn't mentioned the possible job with the morning show, but it never was far from Lenae's mind. So much so that she hadn't expected their brief affair to continue once they returned to Washington. She'd prepared herself for a breakup and had heard her own voice grow colder and more distant during the flight home.

Cara had seemed distracted herself, disappearing from Lenae's life for the past week, and Lenae had accepted the inevitable—but quiet and mature—end to their short affair. Cara's call had been welcome, but unexpected. Mostly because Lenae thought their fling was done, but also because she'd never have imagined Cara would invite her to a very public Bradley family event.

❖

Cara pulled up in front of the house and saw Lenae sitting on the porch. She was stunning. Simply dressed, as always, but with a refined elegance that suited her almost-regal, somewhat-serious face and body. Cara had missed that body over the past few days. She'd missed the way Lenae was able to let go of her composure with abandon when they were in private and attuned to one another. She'd missed the moments when she was lying on top of Lenae with their fingers twined together, holding Lenae's hands against the pillow while she kissed her way down Lenae's body. Neither one of them had been able to keep control for long.

Cara got out of the car and straightened her simple black silk tank. She put Pickwick in the backseat, but he jumped into the front again. She left him there, hoping he'd stay put once Baxter was in the backseat with him. She was *not* letting the puppy call shotgun if Lenae was going to be in the car.

"Hey, stranger," Lenae said. She stood when Cara stepped onto the porch. Baxter wagged his tail and grinned at her, and she walked over to give him a pat and Lenae a lingering kiss.

"Hey, yourself. You're beautiful."

Lenae brushed her fingers over Cara's hair and face. "So are you. You're…familiar to me."

Cara inhaled sharply at the words, holding herself still while Lenae touched her even though she wanted to touch Lenae right back. Lenae's exploration of her face and body—begun last week and continued now—had made Cara feel known like never before.

"Thanks for agreeing to go with me tonight." Cara had always felt the need to protect herself from her own dates, never certain of their true motives, the few times she brought women around her family. She wasn't accustomed to having someone who would be able to protect her from their slings and arrows. She smiled and took Lenae's hand as they walked to her car. She let go only long enough to get the dogs situated in the back and the humans up front, and then she linked their hands again and rested them on Lenae's thigh. She felt the security of their connection and a confidence she'd never had when taking a date to one of the many Bradley openings or awards ceremonies or screenings. Lenae was here with her, not using her but *with* her. Cara hadn't ever had such complete faith in another person before.

Lenae held Cara's hand in her left and used the fingernails of her right hand to gently skim over Cara's wrist. "What family members am I going to meet tonight? What are they like?"

"My dad you've met over the phone already," Cara said, as if Lenae needed reminding. "He's a sportscaster, but he did some stage work when he was younger. He met my mom in Ashland, Oregon when he was a regular cast member in the Shakespeare festival there, and she was brought in to do a starring role as Lady Macbeth. He moved with her to Los Angeles and got into the news side of television. They moved to Seattle when Mom was cast in a medical drama filmed around here. It went off the air, but her new sitcom was set in Seattle specifically for her."

Cara's responses were more about their acting careers than about their personalities, but she didn't know any other way to describe them.

"What about your brother?"

"He's brilliant. He followed in Dad's footsteps and did Shakespeare before coming to A Contemporary Theatre in Seattle. He's starred in plenty of plays at ACT, but he's more a playwright and director than actor now, so there's lots of buzz when he's onstage instead of behind the scenes. Mom and Dad pushed him to be a film star, but he loves the theater too much to leave. He's respected and adored, and he cares more about that than making the millions my parents envisioned for him." Cara felt her voice warm a little when she talked about Richard, and she was much more at ease when Lenae changed the subject to the play they were going to see.

"*Mourning Becomes Electra* is one of my favorite plays," Lenae said.

Cara was enjoying the process of shifting from reciting her parents' resumes to a more relaxed state. Just being with Lenae helped ease the knots of tension she felt inside. Lenae's ability to get through to Cara this way was intoxicating.

"Richard adores Eugene O'Neill, so ACT puts on one of his plays every so often as a way to entice him back to the stage. He can't resist, but I believe his real love is writing."

Richard was more capable of breaking away from their parents' expectations than Cara. She sometimes wondered what had been so different between them, but she suspected she cared more about their approval—and disapproval—than he did.

"I considered being a playwright," Lenae said. "But journalism was more my style. Always new, often a crisis. Thinking and learning about each story quickly enough to get it written while it was still relevant was a challenge I loved. But I still feel I have a play inside me, trying to get out. Hopefully, not like *Alien*."

Cara groaned at the image. "With your sense of spatial relations, I'll bet you'd be able to use settings to full advantage.

Sounds, pauses, space. Too many poor playwrights don't pay attention to elements beyond the visual." Cara paused. She knew Lenae wasn't angling for an easy route into the theater world, but her past experiences had left her too jaded not to wonder. Still, she couldn't resist offering Lenae anything she might want. "I'm sure my brother would be willing to talk over some of your ideas, or maybe help you get a play produced somewhere."

Lenae laughed. "I'm sure he has nothing better to do." She squeezed Cara's hand, and Cara felt her tension shatter and blow away. "I appreciate the generous offer of his time, but I haven't written anything yet. First I need to make the center a success, and then *possibly* I'll do some writing in my spare time. I have connections of my own, too, you know. What about you and the stage? You said you used to perform plays, but have you done Shakespeare or O'Neill? Or did you switch to reporting after your parents took the fun out of your impromptu plays?"

"I was advertising detergent and baby food before I could walk, and anytime there was a walk-on part or role for a child, my parents had me in the audition line. I knew my way around a stage, and my teachers in school knew it. I was cast as the lead in school plays even when I didn't audition. I actually liked acting, but I didn't have the same skills my brother did, so by high school I was being groomed to follow in Dad's footsteps and be a news reporter. Doing poorly in any acting role—even a junior high production of *Up the Down Staircase*—was unacceptable to them, so they made me turn down school productions when I wasn't showing enough promise. During college I did a show similar to *Around the Sound* and loved interviewing people and drawing out their stories. I found my niche, I guess. I was better at that than character work. I'm best at playing myself."

"A version of yourself," Lenae said without thinking. She didn't filter her words because she was too focused on the ridiculous notion of dissuading a girl from a hobby she loved just because she might not be a gifted star.

Cara was silent for a moment as they sped along the freeway toward Seattle. "Most people can't tell the difference," she said. "And to be honest, I'm not always certain which is the real me."

"You're not?" Lenae asked in surprise. "I wouldn't have any trouble distinguishing you from your on-air persona. I'll bet if I heard you say a single sentence, both in front of a camera and just in conversation, I'd be able to tell when you were being filmed."

"How?"

Lenae thought about Cara's question, replaying Cara's voice in her mind. "It's more to do with energy than with anything else. When you're being a television reporter, your energy moves outward, toward other people. It draws them to you and might be why your show is so successful at bringing in donations and volunteers. You *include* other people, and your shimmering qualities rub off on them. When you're talking one-on-one, your energy moves inward, as if you're storing up what you experience and feel, pulling it deep inside. You're still the same person, and I like both of you."

Cara paused again. "Sometimes you describe things in ways I've never even considered. I always thought I was being phony on television—even when I truly cared about the topics—because I could keep my voice and body so controlled. I saw it as a shortcoming, a flaw in my character."

Lenae shook her head. "It's a gift."

"Thank you," Cara said finally. Simply.

"For what?" Lenae asked, still drawing circles on Cara's delicate wrist.

"For what you notice in me. For taking the time to feel and understand me." Cara lifted Lenae's hand and kissed her palm. "Now on to a less personal, but no less vital topic, dog whisperer. How the hell can I keep a puppy like Pickwick calm for an entire play?"

CHAPTER TWENTY-THREE

Cara described the set to Lenae in a low voice once the curtain went up, and then she retreated to her private world. She heard Lenae and the rest of the audience responding to the words with gasps or short bursts of laughter, and she forced her attention onto her brother when he was onstage so she'd be able to discuss his performance when she saw him later. But, like Lenae had said about her energy moving inward, Cara was taking Lenae's comments about her and studying them in private.

She had never thought of the change in herself the way Lenae had described. She had thought of herself as superficial, as if putting on an act in front of the camera. But she had to at least consider this different way of viewing herself. When she filmed her show or when she taught classes or documented Pickwick's progress, she really was projecting something. She wanted to reach people in her audience, to share with them something she found important. When she talked to people without the cameras or audience present, she never trusted them to see her—or that there was anything for them to see—so she held part of herself back. Apart. Somehow Lenae had gotten past her barriers, past the walls she had built that were more impenetrable than the camera lens.

Pickwick slept with his head resting on her foot, and she almost dozed off as well. Richard was commanding and powerful as General Ezra Mannon, and the play was a favorite of Cara's as well, but she was too caught in her internal world to fully take part in the production. Intermission caught her by surprise. She blinked in the lights and let go of Lenae's hand to clap while the curtain dropped. "Do you like it so far?" she asked as they stood up and filed out of the box with Baxter in the lead. Maybe Lenae could give her some words to use when Cara was grilled about the play by her parents and Richard. Otherwise, she'd just have to make up some praise based on past productions.

"I do, very much. I knew your brother had talent, but I didn't realize how much. He really becomes the characters he's playing, doesn't he?"

"He's a natural. He used to read to me when I was little, and he'd change with every character in every book. He made stories come alive for me."

Cara saw the crowd of people below them when they reached the staircase leading down to the lobby, and she felt Lenae's hesitation as the throbbing sound of numerous conversations floated up to them. Baxter was close to her side.

"Why don't you stay up here with the dogs?" Cara took Lenae's arm and led her to a bench. "I can get us a couple of glasses of champagne without worrying about Pickwick getting his paws stepped on."

"Baxter and I will be happy to puppy-sit. He's not fond of crowds, either."

Lenae leaned back against the leather seat and Pickwick sat pressed against her leg. She could feel his head turning back and forth as people walked by. She replayed parts of the scenes in her mind, studying the way Richard had interpreted Ezra. She had heard the play a few times before, but he had brought out nuances and shades of tone she hadn't experienced. But even as she admired his skill, she ached for young Cara who hadn't shown the same talents as her precocious older brother. The image of Cara's ashtray, the way she'd been discouraged from acting if she wasn't bound to be a star—the things Lenae had learned about

Cara's childhood ran through her mind, with the background music of Cara singing karaoke with abandon and little concern for the actual notes of the tune. Lenae smiled at the memory of their karaoke night, feeling her face heat as she remembered what had happened after they got back to the hotel, and she started in surprise when a deep voice addressed her.

"You must be Lenae McIntyre."

"What gave me away?" Lenae asked, hoping to cover her embarrassment with a wide smile. "And I recognize your voice. Howard Bradley."

"Pleasure to meet you. May I sit?"

Lenae moved to one side of the bench and Cara's dad sat next to her. He had a presence that was as big and resonant as his voice.

"I saw you and Cara on the morning show last week. You were quite captivating."

"Thank you, but Cara is the on-air talent. I enjoyed doing the show more than I expected, but I'm much happier behind the scenes."

"Cara is a natural. She's a Bradley through and through."

Lenae wondered if it was true. Cara had qualities in common with her famous family, but did she want the same things? What would Howard have said if he had heard his daughter singing off-key in public? Would he have been so quick to claim her as a Bradley, or would he have left the bar?

Howard leaned closer and lowered his voice. He still had the projection needed to broadcast a whisper to a full house. "I know she wanted to break the news to you herself, but I'm such a proud papa that I can't help myself. The producers of *Morning Across America* were so impressed with Cara that they've offered her a position as host of the show."

Lenae forced herself to keep completely still and not move away from Howard. "I heard rumors about that when we were in New York. It's no surprise they'd want her there—her kind of talent would be an asset to any show."

"Good, I'm glad you agree. Let's be honest here. Cara has a promising career ahead of her, and I don't want anything to stand in her way. That includes the pretty guide-dog trainer with whom she's currently enamored."

Lenae frowned at his words. Was he implying *she* would be capable of holding Cara back, if she really wanted to take the new job?

"Um, no…I mean, yes, I agree. I'd never want to stand in the way of something Cara really wanted."

"What a relief to hear you say that." Howard exhaled, and Lenae felt him lean back and drape his arm over the back of the bench. "I was worried you'd hold her to this puppy-walking obligation. I know she promised you a year, but the whole point of the project was to get her noticed by the right people, so there's no sense in her continuing the local news spot when she has a chance to go national."

Lenae forced her body to remain relaxed even as her thoughts tumbled over each other. Howard wasn't worried about her relationship with Cara being enough to keep her from New York. He was only trying to find a way to get Cara out of her year commitment to the center. Apparently, it wasn't conceivable to him that either Lenae or Pickwick would be able to hold Cara down when she was ready to soar.

"Cara hasn't spoken to me about this yet," she said, her voice cold, as if this news meant nothing to her. "But if she needed to move to New York, I'd take Pickwick back and find another puppy walker for him."

"Good to hear." Howard patted her knee and stood up. "Because once she accepts, she'll be starting the new show in two weeks."

"She already accepted?" Lenae couldn't believe Cara would take a job—especially one that meant she'd have to give up Pickwick—without telling her. Or didn't she mean enough to Cara?

"Not that I know of, but how could she refuse? She'll be doing the types of interviews she loves, showcasing people who are working to make the world a better place. She'll be able to reach and influence thousands more people than she could with her little show. You know how much that means to her." He paused. "I'm glad to hear that you don't want to hold her back from fulfilling her potential."

"Never," Lenae said emphatically, the emotion she'd been holding back spilling into her voice. Howard Bradley was right. Cara deserved this opportunity not only for herself but to show her family she was more than a rejected ashtray.

"I hope you enjoy the rest of the play, Ms. McIntyre."

❖

Cara stood in line at the concession stand and watched Lenae on the balcony. She saw her dad approach Lenae and the dogs, and she started to walk back toward the staircase. She wasn't sure what he was about to say, but the last time he had spoken to Lenae, over the phone, he had managed to irritate her and make Cara look like one of the relentless starlets she had used to date. Her mother stopped her with an iron grip on her elbow before she was able to walk away.

"Your friend is quite attractive," Lydia said, following Cara's gaze to the balcony. "Even prettier in person than on camera, though. That's a shame."

"She's beautiful either way," Cara said after a pause while Lydia signed an autograph for a young woman. Public conversations with her mother were always broken up by photo ops and frantic searches for pen and paper.

"An interesting dalliance for you, I suppose, but hardly the type of woman with whom you'll want to form a lasting connection."

"You don't know me, Mother," Cara said as she inched forward in line. She looked up at Lenae and saw her father rest his arm along the seat back in his carefully orchestrated relaxed pose. His showmanship would be lost on someone like Lenae, whether or not she was able to see it. She'd see right through it. "Maybe Lenae is exactly the kind of woman I've been searching for all my life."

Lydia gave a derisive laugh. "A dog walker? Really, Cara, think about your future. Your father and I can only do so much for your career. At some point you have to take responsibility for yourself."

"She's a dog *trainer*. And I take responsibility for everything in my life. Pickwick, my students, my show. They're what matter to me. And Lenae does, too."

"Honestly, Cara, I don't understand what's going on in that pretty little head of yours. If you want to get ahead in this business, you need to surround yourself with people who will propel you forward, not drag you back. If she were still with Three-N, or if she had some salvageable connections, maybe I could see it…"

"Maybe I don't want to get ahead. At least not the way you expect from me—"

"Shh, darling…" Lydia turned to greet another fan. "Of course I'd *love* to sign your program. Are you enjoying my son's show? He always brings a tear to my eye when I see him on-stage, but I guess that's because I'm a sentimental mother at heart."

Cara rolled her eyes like a petulant child and ordered two glasses of champagne. She needed to get away from Lydia and rescue Lenae from Howard.

"Thanks for the advice, Mom," she said when the fan left. "But I think I know who's best for me, not just for my career."

"Unlikely, if I look at the choices you've made so far. Have your fling with the dog groomer, but be ready to leave her behind. You'll meet plenty of interesting women who will not only be potential lovers but will bring the right connections along with them."

Cara picked up the flutes and walked away without another word, not even bothering to correct her mother's obviously intentional denigration of Lenae's career. She walked up the steps to Lenae as quickly as she could without spilling their champagne. Her dad had already left.

Pickwick let out an excited yip when Cara returned, but her smile at his enthusiastic response faltered when she saw the expression on Lenae's face. Lenae accepted the glass Cara handed her.

"Sorry, I was waylaid by my mom. And I saw you had the dubious good fortune of being entertained by my dad while I was gone."

"Yes, dubious," Lenae said. Cara sat close enough beside her to feel the tension rippling through Lenae's body. "He said you were offered a job with the morning show."

"Oh, well…yes, I was. I was going to tell you, but…I'm sorry he said something before I did." She had wanted to be with Lenae tonight. The job offer had nothing to do with the two of them, and she hadn't found a good time to bring it up. She hadn't wanted to bring it up, ever.

"So am I," Lenae said, her voice sounding distant and empty. She shifted slightly away. "You'll need to give Pickwick back to the center. Our puppies have to stay in the area."

"I never said I was taking the job," Cara said. Her voice sounded cold and unfamiliar to her own ears. Not like her on-air persona or her normal self, but someone empty. "I have so much to consider. Pickwick and my teaching job. My show. Us." How could Lenae think she'd leave?

"It'd be a shame to give up this opportunity." Lenae echoed Howard's words. "I know how important it is for you to use your talent to promote places like my center. If you have the chance to do this on a national level, I think you should take it."

Cara took a sip of her champagne, willing herself not to cry. "Well, then, maybe I will."

CHAPTER TWENTY-FOUR

Cara sat in a darkened room in the communications building, splicing together clips from family home movies, television commercials, and still photos of her home and relatives. Each of her students was creating a personal biography exploring the roots of their cultural and personal values, and Cara needed to walk them through the editing process with her own segment. She wanted to delete some of the footage, and she still wasn't convinced she'd let her own life story be included in the final class project, to be publicly screened, but she wanted to face her past and her roots with as much honesty as she could muster. She watched scene after scene from her life, mentally picking and choosing among the images while physically sitting on her hands whenever she was tempted to leave out episodes she found too revealing or personal. She expected her class to approach this final project with integrity and vulnerability, and she had to do the same. Years of careful control in front of the camera were hard to break, however, and she had a difficult time resisting the need to manage the images she would be projecting on screen.

Cara watched some of her favorite segments of *Around the Sound*. She'd filmed artists and musicians who were spreading messages of hope, Tess and her efforts to raise awareness of the local marine life, wildlife sanctuaries, and animal rescue groups. And Lenae. Cara replayed the raw footage from the center and listened to her own words as she subtly criticized the people who volunteered as puppy walkers. She finally heard what she had really been saying about the coldness of her own family and about her inability to truly believe that people really existed who lived with love as their overarching value. She looked down at Pickwick, lying at her feet and chewing on an old cassette tape. She'd almost missed out on having him in her life, and having Lenae in her life, because of the beliefs she'd developed as a child.

She pried the tape out of Pickwick's mouth and gave him a chew toy instead. Maybe people were not formed only by the influences in their lives, but also by the ways they rejected those influences. By learning better and different ways. She had been looking at the world in black-or-white terms. Either she was a media personality or a person of substance. She never believed it was possible to be both at once, until Lenae. Lenae had taught her different ways of defining herself.

She cleaned up her workspace and attached Pickwick's leash to his collar just as the class started filing into the room. She raised the lights a little but left an image of her as a child on the screen, smiling widely as she held a spoonful of soup. The screen capture from one of her first ad campaigns seemed to capture her childhood. She was always selling something. Herself, her looks, her soul. But she had since proved that she could be on-camera, and enjoy being on-camera, without losing any of her integrity or character. She had compared herself—never favorably—to the people she spotlighted on her show, but in her own way and with her own unique talent she was doing good work. She had gained new understanding with Lenae's help, but now she had lost Lenae.

"We've studied roots and their influences from a distance this semester," she said, once all the students had arrived and settled into seats. "What makes people tick. What gets them out of bed in the morning or drives them back into it at night. I asked you all to bring an object from your past today, something that has defined you in some way. I'll start with mine, and then I'd like everyone to share their own stories."

Cara clicked through several images on screen, each showing her with a big smile, a happy family, a warm and loving façade. After a few slides, she held up the ashtray from her desk. It had been such a fixture in her offices and apartments over the years, she might not have chosen it as a significant memento in her life if it hadn't been for Lenae. "I made this for my dad when I was in elementary school. As you can see from my photos, my family appeared to have everything. A glamorous lifestyle, affluence, fame, cute kids…"

Cara paused as the class laughed at her falsely modest tone. She smiled and continued. "But under the surface, there wasn't any real affection or love. There was coldness, distance. Approval when I said or did the right thing at an audition and got a part, but no real tenderness when I didn't. I've carried this ashtray with me my whole life—even before I was consciously aware of what it represented—because I felt the significance of the rejection of this birthday gift intuitively as a child, and more overtly as an adult."

She paused, hating to tell the story but needing to get it out. "My dad opened the box and laughed. He said he already had a gold-plated ashtray for cigars that matched his office, and besides, I had made the indentations too small. Because the appearance of this ashtray was all wrong, the love and effort I had put into it weren't important at all. I learned a lesson that day—one that was reinforced throughout my childhood—and this small piece of clay symbolizes the way I've seen myself, the way I react to the world around me. Only by accepting the pain, acknowledging it and letting it go, can we move forward and start to reconstruct new roots, and new branches into the future."

Cara sat and invited the students to share their objects and stories. As she had hoped, they took a cue from her blatant honesty and matched it with their own. She was accustomed to getting the people she interviewed to open up by mustering her acting skills and keeping the focus on them, not herself. She had never encouraged openness in others by opening up herself, except with Lenae. There was something freeing about it, and she felt the release ripple through her classroom. Some of the students talked about what they had brought to class—articles of clothing handed down through generations, books and journals, photos—but some of them admitted that the real truth was still hidden at home. That they had brought something to complete the class assignment, but if they were going to be completely honest, they should have brought something entirely different.

Cara turned the ashtray over and over in her hands. She remembered the pain of her dad's rejection as if it had just happened, but it was only a shadow of the loss she had felt when Lenae had walked away from her at the theater. She had poured her child's heart into making the gift for her dad, but how much more of herself had she given to Lenae? Everything she was, and the rejection was so much worse because of it.

Cara listened and prompted, falling back into her role of interviewer with ease and relief. She'd honor the stories her students were sharing by including her own personal history in the final film. She wouldn't invite her family to watch—they wouldn't understand. But she'd invite Lenae. She might not come, but Cara was truly telling the story for her ears.

CHAPTER TWENTY-FIVE

Lenae was back in Seattle the following weekend, leading her group of students and their dogs on a field trip. The memory of being here with Cara, sharing a romantic date with her only to have it end in heartbreak, was too fresh in Lenae's mind. She had made an excuse of a splitting headache—not far from the truth—and had left before that fateful intermission was over. Cara hadn't tried to stop her, and Lenae and Baxter had walked the familiar route to the bus stop, calling Des for a ride home from Tacoma.

A few days later, Cara had returned the favor by claiming to be sick for their puppy-walking class. Truth be told, Lenae had wanted to fake an illness today, so she wouldn't have to walk downtown, near ACT. And so she wouldn't have to deal with Gene and Toby.

The other new handlers were doing well, and she wished she could focus on the two success stories and not her one glaring failure. She had reworked the pairings in her mind, wondering if Gene would have done better with one of the other dogs. Or maybe she should have rejected his application in the first place. But she'd thought he'd be a good candidate, and she'd been so certain he and Toby would find a real bond together.

She and Des had mapped out a series of tests for the students. They were riding the bus together from Olympia to Seattle, and from there they'd split up and go on a scavenger hunt of sorts. The new handlers each had to collect items from several stores in the downtown area, proving they were able to maneuver through crowded streets, find unfamiliar locations, and handle public transportation.

At least the exercise would help distract her from thoughts of Cara. She was confused by what had happened between them. Why Cara's dad had told her about the morning show job, instead of Cara herself. Why Cara had sounded uncertain about the move, as if she was really considering turning it down. Lenae had been too angry, too hurt, too caught off guard, to question Cara at the time. Instead, she had basically told her to leave. Of course, it hadn't been difficult to convince Cara, and Lenae figured she was following the plan she'd had in mind all along.

But none of that explained why Cara had invited Lenae to the viewing of her class project. Lenae wasn't sure she'd be able to sit in the screening room, listening to Cara's sweet voice, remembering her honey taste, and then walk away again. It had taken all her resolve to tell Baxter to take her away from the theater, away from Cara.

Lenae followed Baxter off the bus when they got to her stop. Each of the students had a different assigned stop, and Des would keep track of them throughout the day. Lenae told Baxter to go to Pike Place Market and he set off without hesitation. She tried to console herself as they walked. At least Cara hadn't been like Traci. Cara hadn't intentionally used Lenae, even though Cara's promos for the center had been instrumental in getting her the new position. Cara had even brought up Lenae and their relationship as a reason to stay, but Lenae couldn't take that protestation seriously. How quickly Cara would come to resent her if Lenae held her back. Howard had been right about that, at least.

As much as she hated to admit it, Lenae had to agree with Howard about Cara, although his motives were more connected to control of Cara's career and promoting his family name than concern for his daughter. Lenae only cared about Cara's heart. She had been cold and pushed Cara away, but only because she recognized what a talent she was. Beautiful inside and out. Lenae had no doubt Cara would use this new opportunity to do good in the world, to share bigger and more influential stories. Lenae was dying inside, but she wouldn't be selfish enough to deny Cara this chance to grow.

Baxter maneuvered through the crowds with a waving tail and perked ears. She felt his happiness through the harness. She had been at home too much this week, consoling herself with unhindered movement through her apartment and self-pitying meals alone. But she needed to get back in the world, for Baxter if not for herself. He loved the excitement of city streets and fascinating scents. They made quick time to Pike Place, and she was almost at the store where she liked to buy her favorite tea when her cell vibrated. Des. She answered with a sigh.

"Problems already?" she asked.

"Yeah. You-know-who is at Starbucks next to Westlake Center. He says this is a stupid game and he's not interested in playing."

"Great. Go ahead and follow the others. I'll handle Gene."

Lenae disconnected and gave Baxter their new destination, which was close to their point of origin. She had walked all that way just to have to turn around again. By the time she reached the coffee shop, she was fuming. Cara was leaving her and abandoning Pickwick. She was a failure at pairing dogs and owners—a huge part of her job as trainer. And she had worn the wrong shoes for traipsing up and down the hilly Seattle streets.

She sat down at the table once Baxter had led her to Toby. No consoling, no preamble. "What's going on, Gene?"

"I felt like having coffee, so I had Toby find a coffee shop. That seems to be enough proof that we're working together, so why bother doing your little scavenger hunt?"

Lenae was tempted to coax him into trying the activity. To somehow get through to him that life would be better once he accepted his changed circumstances. But she didn't believe her own reassurances any more. She thought back to Cara's comment about acknowledging and allowing Gene's anger.

"Fine," she said. "You're right, you don't have to do the exercise."

"Really? Well, good." She heard the surprise in Gene's voice. She had expected to hear relief as well, but she wondered if he was trying to goad her into an argument so he could vent his anger somehow.

"Good," she repeated. "Once we get back to the center, Toby will stay with us and you can pack your bags and leave."

Silence. "But I need him…we've been working fine…you can't just—"

"Yes, I can. It's in the contract you signed. Until you graduate from the training program—and even after that, if I think Toby is in any danger with you—I can take him back."

"But he's not in danger." Gene's voice grew louder and Lenae heard the shock in his tone. "I'd never hurt him."

"Maybe not directly, but you're too angry to be kind to him. You both are doing the basics, but you're not connecting. That's not fair to Toby. He deserves to be a loved and cherished member of a team, not a tool for you to use."

"What about what's fair for me?"

Lenae wanted to reach across the table for his hand, to relieve some of the pain she heard in his voice. But she kept her distance. Life wasn't fair, damn it. A nice guy like Gene shouldn't have to deal with such a devastating loss, but his accident had happened. She shouldn't have been tempted to fall in love only to have Cara leave, but the opportunity had arrived. "It wasn't fair for you to lose your sight. You have every right to be sad or furious or whatever you need to feel. Your life has been changed forever, and not in a way you chose. But if your emotions are harming Toby by depriving him of the chance to really connect with someone who needs him and will love him, then I'll take him back and give him to someone else. When you figure out how to keep loving even though you're personally in pain, you can reapply for another dog and I'll consider it."

Lenae heard a quiet choking sound from Gene, but she got up and told Baxter to take her back to Pike Place. She'd brave the blisters and sore feet just for a chance to put distance between herself and the hurting man. He had Toby if he wanted comfort, just like she was turning to Baxter now that Cara was gone. She had to let Gene find his own way. Her platitudes didn't do any good, nor did her avoidance of his emotional issues. He either had to take responsibility for his own anger, or he'd have to leave Toby behind.

She walked away from the coffee shop and thought about Cara and her advice about allowing people their emotions instead of telling them how to feel. Had she done the same thing with Cara? Assumed she'd want to leave without giving her a chance to discuss the new job? Howard had assumed she'd want the job and hadn't acknowledged her reasons for possibly wanting to stay. Lenae had done the same thing. She hadn't listened when Cara had hesitated about the job. She'd told her to take it, protecting herself from being left and being hurt instead of paying attention to what Cara might be feeling or wanting.

And now it was too late.

❖

Lenae waited with Des at the bus stop for the students to return. Angela was first, with Corey close behind. Des was going through the small trinkets they had purchased from the assigned stores as proof they'd successfully visited each one, when Gene and Toby stopped next to Lenae.

"We're not too late, are we?" Gene asked, sounding out of breath. He touched Lenae on the forearm and put a small bag in her hand. "We found everything on the list."

Lenae felt the objects in the bag while her heart soared at his use of the word *we*. "Of course you're not too late. Did you have any trouble finding the stores?"

"No, even though I put us behind schedule by sulking in the coffee shop. I told Toby we had to hurry to catch up, and he took off like a shot. Lenae, I know you have every right to take Toby away from me, but please give me another chance. I've been keeping him from getting too close, but I can change. I need him, and I think he needs me, too. Give me another chance?"

Lenae pulled out the dog toy from a local pet store, one of the objects on the scavenger hunt list, and put it in Gene's hand. "Yes, you can have another chance. And Toby can have this for the bus ride home."

"What'd you say to him?" Des asked as they rode back to Olympia. "He looks like a different man. And Toby is back to his happy self."

"I took the advice of a friend," Lenae said. "Instead of telling him everything would be okay, I told him it might not. I guess he needed the honest kick in the pants more than the platitudes."

"Don't we all," Des said. Lenae couldn't have agreed more.

CHAPTER TWENTY-SIX

Cara opened the folding wall and clipped it in place, creating one large room. Her students were already setting up chairs and lowering the huge television screen, so she turned her attention to setting up the table of refreshments. She had originally planned to show the student film in one of the lecture halls, but she was glad she had chosen Evergreen's Longhouse instead. Set back in the woods, the building was one of the most organic and detailed on the campus. The floors were ornate tiles with geometric prints, and cases filled with Native American artifacts lined the hallway. Artwork depicting marine life and animals decorated the walls. Although not representing any specific culture, the building and its decorations evoked a general feeling of tribe and place. An ideal venue for the film.

Cara had invited Lenae to the small screening, but she didn't expect her to attend. Well, maybe she'd come and take Pickwick away from Cara since she was so sure he was about to be left behind. Cara kept him close by her side all evening, just in case. He followed her from task to task, pulling every once in a while as he tried to get attention from one of the kids. Cara mindlessly went about her business, answering questions and giving direction, but her thoughts were all centered on Lenae. Lenae had been hurt that Cara hadn't told her about the job offer immediately, and Cara knew she'd messed up on that score.

But *she* was hurt by Lenae's reaction. Lenae had no reason to jump to the conclusion that Cara would abandon all her responsibilities without hesitation. She'd thought Lenae really knew her, had thought she'd finally found a woman who saw her as worthwhile and more than good bone structure and a pleasant voice. But Lenae's exceedingly low expectations of her demonstrated she'd been as blind to the real Cara as everyone else.

Cara dumped a bag of chips into a serving bowl. She wasn't certain if she'd discovered her own integrity and depth while listening to Lenae's kind words about her, or if she'd started to develop and nurture them because of Lenae. Either way, she was a better person now. Or maybe the same person, but with the confidence of truly seeing herself. Ironic that the person who taught her to respect and value herself no longer seemed able to recognize her as worthy of being valued. Lenae had pegged her from the start as someone who'd do anything to get ahead—including using Pickwick and the center for exposure—but she thought she'd proved those assumptions false. Apparently not. Lenae still was quick to believe Cara would use her and dump her on the way to bigger and better opportunities.

"There'll be nothing left but crumbs if you aren't careful." Tess had walked up behind Cara while she was setting out rows of cookies. Tess took the box from her and carefully stacked the rest of the treats. "Only girlfriend troubles can provoke that particular scowl. Problems with your lovely guide dog trainer? I'll gladly take her off your hands if she's giving you grief."

Cara picked up one of the cookies she'd broken and handed half to Pickwick before eating the rest. "Lenae isn't mine in any sense of the word. But keep your ocean-pruned fingers off her, anyway."

Tess laughed. "Yeah, you don't sound perturbed by her at all. I'll keep my distance, though, until you decide what you really want."

Tess's words caught Cara off guard. What she really wanted. Did she even know? Had she ever known? She finished chewing and reached for another cookie. She had spent most of her life trying to make her parents proud while detesting the way they only responded to her if her looks and voice were right for a part. She had given up on most of the childish need for their approval—but not all of it—and instead had gone through the same tug-of-war within herself, withholding her own self-approval when she used her talent and camera-ready face to accomplish her goals. Lenae had helped her find a way to unite the two sides of herself, to give in to her love of talking and sharing with an audience without condemning herself for feeling happiness or pride when she performed well. In Lenae's opinion, the good Cara did was magnified by her joy of doing it, not diminished by it.

Until Cara was offered a bigger and better job, far away from Lenae's center. How much of Lenae's anger was triggered by Cara possibly leaving Pickwick behind? And how much by the expectation that Cara would so dismissively leave Lenae herself behind, after what they'd shared?

What did she want? She didn't want Tess coming on to Lenae, she was sure of that at least. "Since you're so skilled at setting up buffets, why don't you concentrate on arranging these fruit trays. They'll keep your mind off Lenae."

"Message received," Tess said with a good-natured smile. "No poaching."

Cara gave her friend a quick hug and walked over to the students who were setting up the projection equipment. She went over last-minute details with them, including a long list of potential problems and how to handle them. The seats were filling up fast, but still no Lenae. Cara sighed and went into one of the smaller rooms to change.

❖

"There she is," Des said as he and Lenae walked into the room. "Nope, now she's gone."

"I don't need to talk to her," Lenae told him, swatting him lightly on the arm. "I just want to sit in the back row and hear her film. She worked hard on it, and I'm interested to find out what her students learned in this seminar."

"Yes, it'll be a fascinating and intellectual evening," Des replied in a tone obviously mocking her own. "We'll experience the production without caring one iota about the stunning woman who produced it. Why don't I seat you behind a pillar so no one will know you're here?"

"Behind a pillar will be just fine, smart aleck," Lenae said. She kept her arm linked with Des's while still holding Baxter's harness. She needed the support of both tonight, even though Des had been nagging her to talk things out with Cara for the past two weeks. Lenae had done enough talking. She wanted to hear Cara's story in film—she owed her that much at least—but she didn't need more exposure to Cara in person. She was devastated about Cara leaving, but she had built a curious distance between them already. Whenever she thought of Pickwick without Cara, she started to cry, but she wouldn't shed tears for herself. She was only here because she needed to hear Cara tell her own story, to share the magnitude of her need to please her parents, and to therefore understand why she was moving to take this new job regardless of the connections keeping her in place. Cara wasn't like Traci, only out for herself. Cara was after something much more powerful and elusive, external approval from parents who seemed incapable of giving her any meaningful praise or support.

"Uh-oh, she saw us," Des said. "Sorry I didn't fling you behind the totem pole in time." He raised his voice. "Hey, Cara."

"Hi, Des. Lenae."

Lenae managed to choke out a hello, still shocked by the way Cara's voice saying her name could send an electric charge through her body. The current was too strong to resist, but Lenae had to fight her attraction. Cara was leaving. She was flying off to New York to lose her identity even more in her parents' goals. Lenae had to hope Cara eventually found what she needed.

"I'll find the two of you seats on the aisle so Baxter will have room," Cara said. She touched Lenae's arm and Lenae tried not to flinch because Cara's hand felt too good, too familiar. "I'm really glad you came."

"Me, too," Lenae said, still in her stiff voice. She followed Baxter to the seats Cara had chosen and sat next to Des. He described the room in detail to her, making her feel fully part of the experience and keeping her from doing her disappearing act.

Cara had put them far enough away from the crowd so Des was able to whisper quietly to her through the opening segments. He described the images on the screen while she listened to each student's voiceover. Some of them focused on their family influences, others on cultural ones, but each of them had captured the essence of who they were and what forces—combined with their personal experiences—had shaped them into the young adults they were today. Lenae was impressed by the level of thought and self-reflection each had accomplished. She could almost hear Cara's voice as she worked with her kids, encouraging them to go deeper, to find kernels of truth and meaning in their life histories. Lenae hoped Cara gave herself due credit for leading her class to such a level of honest exploration.

"Here's Cara's segment," Des whispered. "The first picture is her in a detergent ad. She's wearing—"

Lenae put her hand on his arm to stop him. "I'll just listen," she said. Cara had invited her here tonight. Anything she wanted Lenae to know would be there for her to hear.

Cara's voice-over began:

Like the totem pole outside this building, my life has been built in three stages. Foundation. Stretching and growth. Learning to fly.

I was grounded by the influences of my parents, their parents, my extended family. Performers and entertainers, all. Self-worth was defined not by self but by the projection of some other self.

Lenae could imagine the types of pictures on the screen. Cara in cute outfits, holding boxes of cereal or soap for the camera, looking like a small star instead of a real, live child. Family portraits showing big smiles and loving looks, while the reality of coldness and disregard hovered under the surface, unseen. She ached for the little girl who had learned that performance equaled love—but a version of love that lasted only as long as the next television ad.

I rejected those ideals and values, but part of me clung to the past. Rising out of it, taking inborn talent and early training but trying to elevate it into something better. Something to make myself proud, not just my family. But the roots were too ingrained. The more I pulled myself upward, the more I felt bound to repeat the past.

Cara in the middle, caught between the screen world and the real world she was fighting to protect through her show and teaching. Both so fragile. Lenae wasn't sure what images were on the screen, but she thought of Cara filming her *Around the Sound* segment at Lenae's center. Cara struggling to let go of control as Toby led her to Starbucks. Cara voicing her disapproval of puppy walkers in what Lenae now knew was an unusual release of personal opinion. Her impassioned diatribe against what she saw as heartless abandonment. Lenae understood Cara much better now. If she could go back in time, to that day when they sat on the floor of the puppies' enclosure, she'd be able to hear the pain behind Cara's words. She wouldn't have taken the comments so personally, hearing them as criticisms of her own work. Even now, she wanted to find Cara and hold her, just as she wished she'd done back then.

The eagle on top of the totem pole is poised for flight, yet still connected to the past. Talons grip the essential elements of who I am, what I do, what and whom I love, while wings carry me out of the endless cycle of criticism and unworthiness. Not rejecting the past, but grabbing the parts that will help me reach the heights of who I am and who I can be.

The new show? Lenae wondered if stills of Cara and Pickwick on the New York set were on the screen right now.

Did Cara believe the job of host would lay her demons to rest? Would she finally be reaching and helping enough people, with her expanded audience, to make her feel worthwhile? If so, then Lenae had no choice but to support Cara's move.

❖

Cara watched the final images unfold in front of her. Her and Pickwick, both smiling for the camera. A photo one of her students had taken when she was unaware and planting the hanging basket for Lenae. After-the-show shots of her with the Baer kids, muddy and smiling as she planted seedlings on the prairie, laughing with Lenae and the other puppy walkers. Finally, a picture of her and her class, with Pickwick front-and-center.

Cara turned her attention to Lenae when the film ended, and applause broke out in the room. Lenae had given her the wings she needed to break free from her past. Even at the start of this project, Cara had been focused on the past and how it had shaped her. She had learned to look forward instead, to surround herself with a family that would help her shape the future into anything she wanted. Lenae had helped by showing Cara the rightness of using skills she enjoyed to share stories she believed were important, both on her television show and in her classroom. Cara didn't know if Lenae would understand what she had been trying to convey in the film, but she hoped her words were enough.

Lenae and Des slipped out of the room while Cara was being bombarded by the students and their friends and families. Cara was disappointed not to have another chance to talk to Lenae, but she'd see her soon enough at the next puppy class. In the meantime, she shared the thrill of a well-received performance with her students.

Later, while Cara was folding chairs with the rest of her class, she realized she hadn't felt a letdown after filming her part of the project. Her students, the people she spotlighted on her show, even herself—they were making a small part of the world better in their own way. When she first went to Lenae's center, she had wondered whether Lenae might finally be the one to change her mind, to show her there really was hope and love behind the stories she shared. Unexpectedly, amazingly, Lenae had been the one.

CHAPTER TWENTY-SEVEN

Lenae waited impatiently for her puppy-walking class to arrive. The news crew was setting up in the training arena, so she knew Cara wouldn't be canceling again. She listened as the cars drove in, waiting for the distinctive sound of Cara's Toyota to pull into the parking area.

Gene and Toby had made significant improvement in their relationship over the past week. He'd been shaken by the possibility of losing Toby and had been forced to confront the potential results of his anger. He had cared too much for the dog to let him go—and Lenae felt relieved by the validation of her instincts. If Toby and Gene hadn't had the potential to be a strongly bonded pair, then he would have let her take Toby away without trying to change, to fight for him. It would take time, but they were on a better path.

Lenae had given herself the same talk she'd given Gene. She was going to lose Cara if she didn't fight for her. If she didn't get past her own fears, her own struggle to be so independent that she pushed others away. She had to admit she needed and loved Cara if she wanted a chance to be with her. That meant making difficult choices, but the possibility of love was worth it.

Cara still hadn't arrived when it was time to begin, and Lenae wondered if she'd waited too long. Would she go to New York without saying good-bye? Send someone to deliver Pickwick back to the center instead of coming herself?

She started the class, trying to gather her thoughts and focus on the lesson plan. She went through the motions of answering questions and discussing each puppy's past week's experiences, but her thoughts were centered on Cara. Would she arrive soon? Would she be willing to listen to what Lenae had to say? She felt anxious about what she needed to express, the way Cara needed to hear her words. Baxter pressed close as he always did when she was upset, and she felt his change in posture immediately, alerting her to the arrival of Cara and Pickwick. Lenae continued her lecture as if nothing had happened. As if her world hadn't suddenly righted itself.

❖

Cara slipped into the back of the room and sat on the floor. Pickwick strained at his leash, pulling toward Baxter, while the news crew repositioned the camera so it was focused on Cara. She ignored it, only able to concentrate on Lenae. She hadn't spoken to her much since the night of Richard's play, hadn't seen Lenae since her class film. She hadn't realized how much a part of her life Lenae had become until she wasn't there. Everything reminded her of Lenae. Pickwick, the scent of Chanel in her car after their drive to Seattle, even the old ashtray that she'd made for her dad. She was anxious to hear Lenae's comments about the film, but afraid at the same time. What if Lenae hadn't heard what she had been trying to say?

Lenae's lecture was on different ways to keep the puppies entertained when they had a lot of downtime, during workdays or long trips in the car. Cara's solution to Pickwick's boredom was to let him chew on whatever item was nearest at hand and most easily replaced, but of course Lenae had more practical solutions. Cara jotted some of them down in a notebook covered with holes made by Pickwick's teeth. She hoped the marks wouldn't show up on film.

After the lesson, when the other puppy walkers were starting the more informal conversational part of the evening, Cara filmed the main portion of her weekly news spot. Since she'd missed a week of filming, she described going to New York with Pickwick, explaining in detail what it had been like to have a puppy in the airplane cabin and how he had handled the flight and hotel stay. She even shared the story of the karaoke bar, making it funny and light when her memories of being there with Lenae were sultry and warm. She couldn't talk about the trip without memories of her and Lenae tangled together in bed, and she wondered how flushed she looked. She was surprised they didn't stop filming to cover her in concealing powder.

She was about to wrap up the segment when Lenae and Baxter came over.

"Do you mind if I say a few words?" Lenae asked.

"On-camera?" Cara knew Lenae avoided being on-air whenever possible. She'd been wonderful and funny on the morning show, but obviously relieved when the cameras were off again.

"Yes. Please?"

"Of course," Cara said, curious about what Lenae might want to say. "I'll do a quick intro in case there are new viewers who haven't seen the spot before."

Cara introduced Lenae and was about to step out of the shot when Lenae took her hand and kept her close.

"I'm sure many of you saw Cara and Pickwick on *Morning Across America*," she said, facing the camera, but holding tightly to Cara's hand. "The producers of the show, like everyone who watched, were impressed by her. By her beauty and talent. But even more, by her desire to touch the hearts and lives of those who watch her. She's made us proud locally by sharing stories of hope and love on *Around the Sound*, and now she'll have a chance to reach even more people as a host on the morning show."

"But I—"

Lenae squeezed Cara's hand. "Please, let me finish." She turned away from the camera and toward Cara. "When you first came to the center to film, I didn't expect to like you, much less fall in love with you. But I have. Cara, I want to be with you, whether you're here or in New York. I won't stand in the way of your chance to be a national star, but I'd like to share that journey with you."

Cara was speechless as she let Lenae's words settle into her heart. Lenae was as private as Cara's family was public, so for her to broadcast her feelings this way meant more to Cara than she could express. Lenae was stepping into her world, and her actions meant everything to Cara because she understood the effort behind them.

"I don't want you to share that life with me," Cara said. She felt Lenae start to pull away, but she tightened her grip on Lenae's hand. "I don't want that life for myself, either. I never accepted the job in the first place. Everyone just assumed I had, including you."

"But it was such a great opportunity…how could you…?"

"I have what I want right here. My show, my puppy, my students. Most of all, you."

Cara stepped forward and kissed Lenae, expressing everything she couldn't—for once in her life—put into words. Love and gratitude and hope. Pickwick jumped on her leg, wanting to be part of the action, and she and Lenae broke apart, laughing.

"You love me?" Lenae asked, laying her hand on Cara's cheek.

"I love you," Cara said, kissing her again.

"And that's a wrap." The producer shut off the camera with a smile. "Let's give these two some privacy."

❖

Cara sang out, loudly and off-key, as Lenae led her through her tidy apartment, like she had so long ago when she came to tell Lenae she didn't want to be a puppy walker. She hadn't thought the day would end, with all the congratulations and comments from

Des, the training class, and the television crew. Finally, everyone had gone home and Lenae and Cara were alone. Together.

Lenae reached for Cara's shirt buttons, but Cara grabbed Lenae's hands and held them still. "You were really going to move to New York with me? Give up your center and your five-year plan?"

Lenae smiled. "You're my new long-term plan. I'd have made it work. As long as I was with you, nothing else mattered."

Cara marveled at the words. The hurt was still present, but the joy of hearing Lenae say she loved her was beginning to eclipse the pain.

Lenae stopped struggling to get at Cara's shirt buttons and sat on the edge of her bed. "I never wanted to stand in your way. Or worse, to have you stay here because you felt obligated to take care of Pickwick. Or me."

Cara had to laugh at that. She sat next to Lenae and brushed her hair off her forehead. "Me? Take care of you? I think it's the other way around, love. You're the organized one, and I'm a mess. You'll be tripping over me, Pickwick, and all my books so much that you'll buy me a plane ticket to New York just to get me out of your hair."

"Never," Lenae said. She took hold of Cara's hand and kissed the tips of her fingers, her palm, her wrist. She let go of Cara's hand and started undoing her buttons, one by one. "Baxter will lead me around the piles of books and papers. I plan to trip over you for the rest of my life."

Cara put her hands behind her and leaned back, arching upward when Lenae's mouth closed over her nipple. "I understand why you were trying to let me go," she said. "But what made you change your mind?"

Lenae lifted her mouth briefly. "Your project," she said, sliding her fingers under the waistband of Cara's jeans. "The last part of it."

"I was hoping you'd…get what I was trying to tell you, even if you couldn't see the pictures." Cara's sentence was punctuated by a sharp intake of breath when Lenae unbuttoned her jeans for better access. Lenae's hand pressed against her firmly, and Cara lifted her hips to get closer.

"Des was describing everything in your film, but I told him to stop at the end because I didn't want to hear about pictures of you moving forward with your new life. I was hurt because I thought you were leaving, but I realized I wanted to be part of your future, no matter where it took us."

Cara bit her lip and moaned as Lenae's fingers slid under her panties and easily through her wetness. "The pictures weren't of a new job. They were of me and Pickwick. My students, the people I've interviewed on my show. Us. You're my future, and I wanted you to know that."

"You had a picture of me in there?" Lenae asked, her fingers growing still. "Maybe it wouldn't have taken me so long to tell you I loved you if I'd known that. But I hadn't realized how much I did love you until I knew what I was ready to give up to be with you."

"Please don't stop," Cara said, reaching for Lenae's hand and moving it against her. "You're not an obligation, and you're not a pawn to be moved around at my whim. We're in this together, and decisions about moving and jobs will be made for and by both of us."

"I love you," Lenae said, nibbling on Cara's neck as her fingers moved rapidly over her clit.

Cara sang while she still had breath.

CHAPTER TWENTY-EIGHT

Cara sat in a folding chair on the center's green lawn. Pickwick was quietly lying underneath, his nose and paws tucked in as much as his big Labrador body would allow. Des sat next to her, and an assortment of other people filled the three rows of chairs.

Cara tilted her face toward the fading October sun and listened to Lenae talk about dogs and training, but the words slipped right through her. Even when she was sad, even after more than a year of loving Lenae every night and day, she still got as wet and excited as an eager adolescent at the sound of Lenae's throaty voice. Only Pickwick's cold nose against her ankle kept her grounded in this moment and not moving ahead in a fantasy she'd make come true as soon as she and Lenae were alone.

She opened her eyes again. The desire to escape the emotions of today was strong, but she wanted to be present. To feel everything as deeply as she could. She had worked toward this day with all her heart, just as Lenae and the six students on chairs behind her had. They ranged in ages from twenty-two to fifty-one, but all had the same eager smiles. They sat by themselves, white canes gripped in their hands. Alone for the last time.

The man sitting next to Cara—one of the husband-and-wife pair that had puppy walked Pickwick's sister—reached over and took her hand. She looked down the aisle and saw they were all linked together, from the 4-H kids to her, all bonded by this experience. She had learned a lot about them while they had been in classes together. After the news cameras had shut down and the formal class had ended, they'd talk about their homes and lives and how these puppies and this experience had changed them. Always knowing this day was coming.

They went up to the podium one by one, until only Cara and Pickwick were left. She watched Lenae's face transform when she called Cara's name, with the telltale sideways smile and faint blush Cara recognized as meant for her alone. The signs were brief and quickly smoothed into a neutral expression, but Cara saw them and they gave her the strength she needed to get up and walk to the makeshift stage. Pickwick walked calmly at her side, only pulling forward when he saw his new handler waiting for him.

Cara put Pickwick's leash into Elizabeth's hand and gave her a hug before stooping to hug Pickwick's furry neck. She somehow made it back to her seat and through the rest of the ceremony, but she escaped as soon as Lenae made her closing remarks and the families swarmed to congratulate the graduating class of students. Lenae had insisted that this symbolic handing over of the puppies-now-dogs was an important way to say good-bye, but Cara wasn't sure. She'd have to trust Lenae's judgment—as she had learned to do without question—and wait to find out if she really did get a sense of closure from the day. Because right now, she just felt very sad.

Pickwick still exploded into a flurry of puppy joy whenever she approached him, and Lenae reassured her that Baxter always did the same thing when he was reunited with his puppy walker, but a shift had taken place partway through the past months of training. After working with Elizabeth for a few weeks, Pickwick had suddenly, inexplicably but undoubtedly, become *hers*. Cara remembered the exact day when he had bounded over to greet her but had returned to touch Elizabeth's hand with his nose every few seconds. Cara had gone back to the house and cried—hating the deep, deep part of her that admitted to wanting Pickwick to fail out of training so he could stay with her. Lenae had been practical and soothing as ever. *Of course you feel that way. Everyone does, and it's perfectly natural and not mean at all. Wanting to hold on while letting him go is a sign of bravery and love.* Cara still had the occasional fantasy of puppy-napping Pickwick and fleeing the country with him, but at least she felt a little less guilty about those thoughts.

"Find Cara." Lenae barely got the words out before Baxter set off and led her away from the crowd and to the quiet of the porch. She felt for the bench and sat next to Cara, pulling her close and feeling the wetness of tears through the fabric of her shirt. For a few moments, they rested in silence, broken only by Cara's occasional sniff, surrounded by the scent of herbs from Cara's growing number of planters.

"You said I'd feel better after today," Cara mumbled against her shoulder.

"No, I said you'd feel some closure. Eventually you'll feel better. And we'll have new crops of puppies coming through the center all the time. Maybe one will connect with you and you'll want to puppy walk again."

"Never." Cara paused and Lenae wondered what was going through her mind. The chewed-up shoes and books? Pickwick's boundless energy and refusal to obey a command until he had heard it a thousand times? Or the fun of having a constant companion, a warm body who never left her side?

"Well, maybe. Someday," Cara said.

Lenae smiled and turned her face to kiss Cara's hair, her ear, along the side of her neck. "Until then, you have me and Baxter. We'll always be here with you."

"Promise?" Cara asked. She kissed Lenae on the lips, sucking on her lower lip as she did.

"I promise," Lenae whispered, giving herself completely to Cara's increasingly insistent teeth and tongue. She felt surrounded by love. Baxter guided her steps, and Cara had come into her life to guide her heart out of the darkness. She'd spend the rest of her life returning the favor.

About the Author

Karis Walsh is the author of several Bold Strokes Books romances, including Rainbow Award winning *Harmony* and *Sea Glass Inn*. She has also written a romantic intrigue, *Mounting Danger*, and several short stories. A Pacific Northwest native and horseback riding instructor, she is now reveling in the heat of Texas with her partner and their numerous animal-kids.

Books Available From Bold Strokes Books

Let the Lover Be by Sheree Greer. Kiana Lewis, a functional alcoholic on the verge of destruction, finally faces the demons of her past while finding love and earning redemption in New Orleans. (978-1-62639-077-5)

Blindsided by Karis Walsh. Blindsided by love, guide dog trainer Lenae McIntyre and media personality Cara Bradley learn to trust what they see with their hearts. (978-1-62639-078-2)

About Face by VK Powell. Forensic artist Macy Sheridan and Detective Leigh Monroe work on a case that has troubled them both for years, but they're hampered by the past and their unlikely yet undeniable attraction. (978-1-62639-079-9)

Blackstone by Shea Godfrey. For Darry and Jessa, their chance at a life of freedom is stolen by the arrival of war and an ancient prophecy that just might destroy their love. (978-1-62639-080-5)

Out of This World by Maggie Morton. Iris decided to cross an ocean to get over her ex. But instead, she ends up traveling much farther, all the way to another world. Once there, only a mysterious, sexy, and magical woman can help her return home. (978-1-62639-083-6)

Kiss The Girl by Melissa Brayden. Sleeping with the enemy has never been so complicated. Brooklyn Campbell and Jessica Lennox face off in love and advertising in fast-paced New York City. (978-1-62639-071-3)

Taking Fire: A First Responders Novel by Radclyffe. Hunted by extremists and under siege by nature's most virulent weapons, Navy medic Max de Milles and Red Cross worker Rachel Winslow join forces to survive and discover something far more lasting. (978-1-62639-072-0)

First Tango in Paris by Shelley Thrasher. When French law student Eva Laroche meets American call girl Brigitte Green in 1970s Paris, they have no idea how their pasts and futures will intersect. (978-1-62639-073-7)

The War Within by Yolanda Wallace. Army nurse Meredith Moser went to Vietnam in 1967 looking to help those in need; she didn't expect to meet the love of her life along the way. (978-1-62639-074-4)

Escapades by MJ Williamz. Two women, afraid to love again, must overcome their fears to find the happiness that awaits them. (978-1-62639-182-6)

Desire at Dawn by Fiona Zedde. For Kylie, love had always come armed with sharp teeth and claws. But with the human, Olivia, she bares her vampire heart for the very first time, sharing passion, lust, and a tenderness she'd never dared dream of before. (978-1-62639-064-5)

Visions by Larkin Rose. Sometimes the mysteries of love reveal themselves when you least expect it. Other times they hide behind a black satin mask. Can Paige unveil her masked stranger this time? (978-1-62639-065-2)

All In by Nell Stark. Internet poker champion Annie Navarro loses everything when the Feds shut down online gambling, and she turns to experienced casino host Vesper Blake for advice—but can Nova convince Vesper to take a gamble on romance? (978-1-62639-066-9)

Vermilion Justice by Sheri Lewis Wohl. What's a vampire to do when Dracula is no longer just a character in a novel? (978-1-62639-067-6)

Switchblade by Carsen Taite. Lines were meant to be crossed. Third in the Luca Bennett Bounty Hunter Series. (978-1-62639-058-4)

Nightingale by Andrea Bramhall. Culture, faith, and duty conspire to tear two young lovers apart, yet fate seems to have different plans for them both. (978-1-62639-059-1)

No Boundaries by Donna K. Ford. A chance meeting and a nightmare from the past threaten more than Andi Massey's solitude as she and Gwen Palmer struggle to understand the complexity of love without boundaries. (978-1-62639-060-7)

Timeless by Rachel Spangler. When Stevie Geller returns to her hometown, will she do things differently the second time around or will she be in such a hurry to leave her past that she misses out on a better future? (978-1-62639-050-8)

Second to None by L.T. Marie. Can a physical therapist and a custom motorcycle designer conquer their pasts and build a future with one another? (978-1-62639-051-5)

Seneca Falls by Jesse Thoma. Together, two women discover love truly can conquer all evil. (978-1-62639-052-2)

A Kingdom Lost by Barbara Ann Wright. Without knowing each other's fates, Princess Katya and her consort Starbride seek to reclaim their kingdom from the magic-wielding madman who seized the throne and is murdering their people. (978-1-62639-053-9)

Season of the Wolf by Robin Summers. Two women running from their pasts are thrust together by an unimaginable evil. Can they overcome the horrors that haunt them in time to save each other? (978-1-62639-043-0)

The Heat of Angels by Lisa Girolami. Fires burn in more than one place in Los Angeles. (978-1-62639-042-3)

Desperate Measures by P. J. Trebelhorn. Homicide detective Kay Griffith and contractor Brenda Jansen meet amidst turmoil neither of them is aware of until murder suspect Tommy Rayne makes his move to exact revenge on Kay. (978-1-62639-044-7)

The Magic Hunt by L.L. Raand. With her Pack being hunted by human extremists and beset by enemies masquerading as friends, can Sylvan protect them and her mate, or will she succumb to the feral rage that threatens to turn her rogue, destroying them all? A Midnight Hunters novel. (978-1-62639-045-4)

Wingspan by Karis Walsh. Wildlife biologist Bailey Chase is content to live at the wild bird sanctuary she has created on Washington's Olympic Peninsula until she is lured beyond the safety of isolation by architect Kendall Pearson. (978-1-60282-983-1)

Windigo Thrall by Cate Culpepper. Six women trapped in a mountain cabin by a blizzard, stalked by an ancient cannibal demon bent on stealing their sanity—and their lives. (978-1-60282-950-3)

The Blush Factor by Gun Brooke. Ice-cold business tycoon Eleanor Ashcroft only cares about the three Ps—Power, Profit, and Prosperity—until young Addison Garr makes her doubt both that and the state of her frostbitten heart. (978-1-60282-985-5)

Slash and Burn by Valerie Bronwen. The murder of a roundly despised author at an LGBT writers' conference in New Orleans turns Winter Lovelace's relaxing weekend hobnobbing with her peers into a nightmare of suspense—especially when her ex turns up. (978-1-60282-986-2)

The Quickening: A Sisters of Spirits Novel by Yvonne Heidt. Ghosts, visions, and demons are all in a day's work for Tiffany. But when Kat asks for help on a serial killer case, life takes on another dimension altogether. (978-1-60282-975-6)

Smoke and Fire by Julie Cannon. Oil and water, passion and desire, a combustible combination. Can two women fight the fire that draws them together and threatens to keep them apart? (978-1-60282-977-0)

Love and Devotion by Jove Belle. KC Hall trips her way through life, stumbling into an affair with a married bombshell twice her age. Thankfully, her best friend, Emma Reynolds, is there to show her the true meaning of Love and Devotion. (978-1-60282-965-7)

The Shoal of Time by J.M. Redmann. It sounded too easy. Micky Knight is reluctant to take the case because the easy ones often turn into the hard ones, and the hard ones turn into the dangerous ones. In this one, easy turns hard without warning. (978-1-60282-967-1)